Praise for
Walk the Wild Road

"Nigel Hinton is an inspired storyteller. Leo's walk along the wild road will captivate you as it did me. This is a wonderful tale!"

—Bernard Cornwell, international bestselling author of historical fiction

"This is an uplifting, touching, and at times heart-wrenching novel that addresses the issues of class and religious discrimination as well as poverty."

—*School Library Journal*

"A gripping, epic tale of one brave boy's journey into his own future. Leo is an immigrant Huckleberry Finn lighting out for the territories, in this case America itself. *Walk the Wild Road* is a million stories distilled into an adventure you won't forget."

—Wesley Stace, aka John Wesley Harding

"I've just done something I've never done before in half a century in publishing: sat down and read a story from first to last all in one session. *Walk the Wild Road* is more than a page-turner, it's a grip-you and hold-you yarn all the way from its opening paragraph. I feel I could walk in young Leo's footsteps every inch of the way from central Poland to the Baltic shore—and I'm sure I'd be looking over my shoulder every other step to avoid the perils that beset him and his companions in this most gripping and moving, story."

—Malcolm MacDonald, author

Walk the Wild Road

Walk the Wild Road

Nigel Hinton

sourcebooks
jabberwocky

Published by Sourcebooks Jabberwocky, an imprint of Sourcebooks, Inc.
P.O. Box 4410, Naperville, Illinois 60567-4410
(630) 961-3900
Fax: (630) 961-2168
www.jabberwockykids.com

Library of Congress Cataloging-in-Publication Data

Hinton, Nigel.
  Walk the wild road / Nigel Hinton.
    p. cm.
  Summary: In war-torn Poland in 1870, ten-year-old Leo, the oldest of nine children
of impoverished parents, sets out to earn a living, hoping one day to help his family
by making his fortune in America.
  [1. Conduct of life—Fiction. 2. Voyages and travels—Fiction. 3. Family life—
Poland—Fiction. 4. Emigration and immigration—Fiction. 5. Dogs—Fiction. 6.
Poland—History—1864–1918—Fiction.] I. Title.
  PZ7.H5974Wal 2011
  [Fic]—dc22

                              2009032443

Source of Production: Sheridan Books, Inc., Chelsea, Michigan, USA
Date of Production: November 2010
Run Number: 14028-PB/14027-HC

          Printed and bound in the United States of America.
              SB 10 9 8 7 6 5 4 3 2 1

For Roger and Heather Daltrey—

With thanks for the great time in Waterloo Barn,
where this book was written.

Preface

There is a legend in my family that in 1870, when my grandfather was eleven years old, he left his home in a small village in Poland. He was the eldest of nine children in a poor peasant family, and he knew that his parents could no longer support him. Alone, he set out to make his fortune.

This is not his story, but it could have been.

Introduction

In 1870, Poland did not exist. It had been divided up among three countries—Prussia, Austria, and Russia. The action in this story takes place in the section occupied by Prussia. At the time, Prussia was ruled by King Wilhelm I. His minister-president, Bismarck, was intent on challenging the power of France, so Leo's journey took place across a land that was preparing for war.

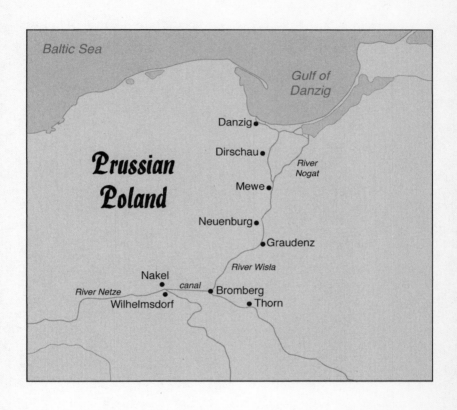

PART ONE

Home

Chapter 1

L EO WAS THE FIRST TO SEE THE STORKS.
    He was on the high bank overlooking his house when
he heard the flapping of wings. He looked up through the bare
branches of the birch trees and saw the big birds overhead. They
were flying low, as if they were going to land.

He held his breath and prayed, "Please stop. Please stay."

At that moment, as though answering his prayer, one of the
storks turned its head and glanced at the stork pole that stood
invitingly at the edge of the village. But the birds flew on across the
track and away over the fields toward the River Netze. He watched
until they were just distant black dots. Then they made a slow turn
to the left and Leo's heart began to beat faster as the dots grew
larger. He realized that they were coming back.

As the storks approached the village again he stood stock-still,
fearing that a sudden movement might scare them away. He became
aware of all the noises around him—a dog barking near the church,
some young children shrieking and calling from the fields—noises
that might frighten the storks.

But no, they kept coming, heading toward the stork pole, a tall
pine trunk with an old cartwheel on the top. His father had built it
eleven years earlier to give thanks for Leo's birth and to attract good
luck for his family and the whole village. Everyone knew that a
stork nest could bring harmony and fertility—babies, good crops,

and healthy animals. But for all of Leo's life, the stork pole had remained empty. And instead of plenty, there had been struggle and scarcity. For three years in a row, the potato crop had failed and famine had gripped the village, carrying off the weak, young and old, with sleeping sickness. Even in the better years, not a belly in the village was ever full.

Only last year, Papa had stopped the whole family near the pole as they were walking home from the funeral of baby Karolina. He had looked up at the chattering magpies standing on the top of the pole and said, "I should take it down and burn it for all the good it has done us. Babies it brings us, only to watch them starve."

But he had not carried out the threat, and now there were storks flying toward the pole. Leo closed his eyes, willing them to land, and his heart thudded in his chest.

When he finally dared to look, the storks were perched on either side of the cart wheel. They stretched out their long necks and began to make a loud, dry, clacking noise with their beaks as if to announce their arrival and their intention to stay.

And stay they did.

Chapter 2

PATIENTLY, TWIG BY TWIG, THE STORKS BUILT THEIR NEST across the cartwheel. People called them "Leo's storks," and the whole village was filled with hope. Within days the weather grew warmer and it felt as if spring had come early.

Every dawn, as Leo and his young brothers herded the geese and the sheep out into the fields, he checked to see that the storks were still there. The large nest looked like a halo around the top of the pole, and he came to think of it as a holy thing. This year would be a good year. There would be food on the table. And even little Jozef would grow strong.

From the moment Jozef was born, Leo had felt a special link with him. He had been a sickly baby, and only Leo had been able to calm him when he cried with the pain of his wheezing lungs. Everyone had said that the little boy was not long for this world, but Leo had willed his tiny brother to live. He had carried him and sung to him and cuddled him at night on the mattress he shared with his brothers and sisters, covering him with his own sheepskin waistcoat against the cold drafts.

Jozef had survived to see his first birthday, and then his second. Whenever Jozef had been ill, Leo had gone out into the woods and fields searching for wormwood and wild thyme to make the herbal teas that the old women of the village said were good for weak chests. And now, Jozef was five. He was still thin and too weak to follow his brothers out into the fields, but Leo had told him that his job was to stay at home and guard the chickens against rats and foxes. So the little boy sat by the window or, if the sun was warm enough, outside on the step of the house, watching the chickens in the yard. And every evening he would proudly show Leo the eggs he had found and tell him that all the chickens were safe.

The good weather held, and people smiled. The storks had brought luck. That's not all they brought.

Mama served the cabbage soup one evening and then, as everyone began to eat, she said, "It's true about storks—for I am to have another baby."

"Really?" Jozef asked, smiling. "A baby!"

"Yes, another mouth to feed," Papa muttered grimly, and everybody stopped eating as he sighed deeply and tugged at one side of his moustache.

Then, after a moment, he opened his eyes and surprised them by winking and chuckling. "But we will endure, won't we? We always endure." He looked at the children, pretending to count them off on his fingers. "So, there will be nine again. That's a good number, don't you think, my little Jozef? A lucky number. And Leo's storks will look after the harvest. Eh, Leo?"

Leo smiled shyly and saw Jozef looking at him, his eyes shining with love.

"Oh, do the stork, Leo," his sister Dorota said, nudging him. "Oh, go on, it's so funny."

"Yes, yes, the stork!" the others shouted, and they began banging on the table. Even Papa joined in.

So Leo jumped up on the bench. He stood on one leg, just like the storks sometimes did, and peered around as if he were looking down a long beak. Dorota and Mama started to giggle. Then, suddenly, he stretched out his neck, waved his arms like wings, and did a perfect imitation of the clacking sound. The little twins, Frederyk and Helena, shrieked and ran to hide in Mama's arms, but a moment later they looked up and joined in the laughter and cheers.

The sunny days lasted until the end of March. Then a bitter east wind brought iron gray clouds and snow. The cold felt cuttingly cruel after the warmth, and soon the promise of spring was buried under a meter of snow. The storks left the nest and flew to the banks of the River Netze, where they were seen sheltering under a bush. Some people said that storks never returned to an abandoned nest, but Leo wouldn't let his hope die—they would be back, and it would be a good year.

Then the disasters struck.

First, Papa found that rats had gotten into the store and had eaten all the seed potatoes he had been keeping for planting. Then, two days later, they lost all their chickens and geese.

They came back from church and found the door to the little poultry shed open. Feathers and blood stained the snow in the yard. A raid by foxes or wolves? Then they saw the footprints—heavy, studded boots. Papa and Leo traced them across the fields. Six pairs of footprints there were, with drops of blood splattered alongside.

"Gypsies or peddlers," Papa said.

But he was wrong. When they got to the river, the footprints were lost in a broad road of trampled snow. They followed the drops of blood and, around a bend in the river, they came upon the army camp. Tents had been pitched in neat rows. Dozens of horses were tethered next to wagons, and at regular intervals, fires had been lit. Cooking pots steamed over the fires, and soldiers stood around them, talking and laughing.

It was obvious what had happened, and even the major they spoke to didn't bother to deny it. He just shook his head and smiled when Papa urged him to search for the thieves.

"I have over eight hundred men here," the major said. "Am I to question every one of them? Besides, King Wilhelm needs them to protect our border with France. You wouldn't want them turning up hungry, would you?"

The major tried another weak smile, but Papa ignored it and strode away.

"The wind always blows in the face of the poor," Papa muttered as they tramped back across the frozen fields. "The wind always blows in the face of the poor. And they can do anything to us, Leo, anything."

When they got back with the news, Jozef broke down and sobbed, saying that he should never have gone to church, that he should have stayed at home and guarded the chickens. Leo told him not to worry but he went on crying and Papa suddenly lost his temper.

"Shut that noise!" he shouted, unstrapping his wide leather belt. "Or I'll give you good reason to cry."

Papa had never raised his voice to Jozef before and the little boy gasped and began to cough. The coughing fit went on and on, and Leo took his brother outside and held him tight until it stopped.

That evening Papa got up from his chair and came across to the mattress where Leo and the others were lying. He knelt and, one by one, touched each of them on their head. Last of all, he bent and kissed Jozef's cheek.

Later that night, Leo woke and heard whispering from across the room, where his parents lay on their mattress. He couldn't make out what they were saying until Papa's voice came more loudly, "It must be done."

Then there was silence.

Chapter 3

Papa told them his decision—he was taking the four eldest children to the market in Nakel to find employment for them.

"You boys are good workers," he said to Leo, Alexsy, and Stefan. "There will be farmers or craftsmen looking to hire strong young helpers. They will feed you and lodge you, and pay us a little money. And, for Dorota, we will find a housewife who needs a girl to help with washing and cooking. Perhaps it will be a rich household with carpets and fine china. You would like that, wouldn't you?"

Dorota nodded and tried to smile, but Leo could see the fear in her eyes.

Stefan began to cry and Papa took him by the shoulders. "Come, come, Stefan! You're eight, not a baby. Look at Alexsy. He's only a year older than you, and do you see him crying? It will not be forever. For God's sake, boy, I'm not selling you to a tinker who will take you to the ends of the earth."

On the night before going to the market, Papa went to the tavern and came back smelling of vodka. He tripped as he came through the door and went sprawling on the earth floor.

"The Holy Mother! Look at you," Mama said, as he began to crawl toward the mattress. "What kind of man buys a drink while his family goes hungry?"

"I bought nothing!" Papa said. "My friends paid the rounds out of neighborly love, for my misfortunes."

"You should have asked them for bread, not vodka," Mama insisted. But Papa slumped onto the mattress and did not reply.

Mama came and lay down with the children, with one arm covering Leo and Alexsy, and the other across Stefan and Dorota. As Leo drifted off to sleep, he could hear Mama whispering prayers, and when he woke early the next morning, she was still praying. He knew the prayers were for them, but when it came time to leave she didn't even bid them good-bye. Instead she busied herself with the young children, rolling up the mattress and storing it behind the fireplace. Only Jozef acknowledged their departure. As they walked out the door, he ran across the room and grabbed Leo's hand, holding on tight and kissing it. Leo ruffled his little brother's hair and then stepped out into the freezing dawn.

Papa strode along the track, sometimes so far ahead that they couldn't even hear the crunch of his footsteps on the frozen snow. Leo guessed what he was feeling—the pain and the shame—but he didn't run after him. When Papa's pride was hurt, his anger was never far away.

So Leo stayed with the others. Alexsy was putting on a brave show, boasting as usual.

"I bet I'll be the first to get hired. One look, and they'll see how strong I am. I hope it's for a farmer, but a carpenter or a blacksmith would suit me fine too. Hey, did you know that blacksmiths piss on their hands to toughen the skin? It's true—old Bazyli told me."

"That's why old Bazyli smells so bad," Leo said, hoping to make Dorota and Stefan laugh. But they just trudged on, hand in hand, lost in their fearful thoughts.

Even Alexsy fell silent, so Leo tried again.

"Remember last year when I stayed at the Manor to help with the harvest? The first day I was as scared as a baby rabbit. My heart was going *boom boom*, and I thought I was going to pee myself. Honest! But after that it was fine, and I had a great time."

The words tumbled out of him, but they were all lies. He had hated those six weeks at the Manor. He had been homesick every day and had lived in fear of Borys, the Baron's overseer—a fierce man with hair the color of oxblood—who carried a length of rope that he swung at Leo whenever he was displeased. He was often displeased, and Leo's legs and buttocks had been covered with red wheals.

But worse than Borys was Wolfgang, the Baron's son. He was a year older than Leo, taller, and stronger, and he had a cruel tongue. He knew that Papa owed rent on the farm, and he called Leo "the debtor's son." He made fun of his ragged clothes and bare feet, saying he stank like an animal.

The gloomy memories chilled Leo's heart and stilled his tongue. What if he were to be hired out now to someone even more cruel? A crow flew low across the misty track like the bearer of bad luck, and they walked on in silence.

They were still over a kilometer from town when Dorota stumbled in an icy rut and broke two strips on one of the sandals Papa had woven for her out of birch bark. Dorota put her arm across Leo's shoulder to take the weight off her foot, but by the time they crossed the bridge over the River Netze and reached the outskirts of Nakel, the sandal was falling to pieces.

Papa was waiting for them at the entrance to the market square. He told them to stand near the bakery while he went in search of work for them. Dorota stood with her foot in the air while Leo tried to repair her sandal.

"Hey, you look like a stork on one leg!" Leo joked, trying to cheer her up. She smiled weakly.

He spent a long time weaving the broken strips of bark together but, as soon as Dorota took a step, the sandal came undone again.

"How will I walk home?" she asked.

"We won't be going home. We'll be going with one of them," Alexsy said as he looked nervously at the faces of the jostling strangers in the square, all his boasting forgotten.

Stefan shivered with fear, so Leo took his hand and smiled reassuringly at him.

The hours passed slowly, and they huddled together for warmth. The icy air pinched their faces, and every time the baker's door opened, the smell of bread and cakes teased their empty stomachs. Twice, Papa came back with possible employers. He pointed to each of the boys in turn, saying their names and their ages, but each time the men looked them over and shook their heads.

"The next time, we must smile and stand straight," Leo told the others after the second man had walked away. "We must look strong and willing."

But there wasn't a next time. In the middle of the afternoon the crowds drifted away and the tradesmen began to pack up and leave. Still, Leo and the others waited.

The light was thickening toward dusk when Papa came back with a large woman whose small eyes were almost lost in her fat, red face. She stood in front of them and beckoned to Dorota, who stepped forward, dragging her broken sandal with her foot.

"Does she have a limp?" the woman asked Papa roughly. "I can't be doing with a cripple."

"It's my shoe," Dorota explained.

"Did I ask you?" the woman snapped spitefully.

"No, she's healthy. And strong," Papa said quickly. Then he shot a look at Dorota and added, "Quiet too. And obedient."

"She'll need to be strong if she's to get by in the tavern. The work is heavy," the woman said, feeling Dorota's shoulders and viciously squeezing her arm muscles. "As for obedient, I'll soon make sure of that. Right, I'll take her on the terms we agreed."

She spat on her palm and held it out to Papa. He cast a quick glance at Dorota and shook the woman's plump hand.

The woman pulled some coins out of her purse and gave them to Papa. Then she turned and walked away.

"Forgive me," Papa whispered to Dorota. "Endure. I will bring you home again. I promise."

Then the woman shouted, "Well, come on then!" and Dorota started after her.

She stopped to pick up her broken sandal and, as she stood up again, she glanced back at Leo with a look that stabbed his heart.

They watched until Dorota and the woman turned the corner. Then, without a word, Papa headed across the square. Leo nodded at Alexsy and Stefan, and they followed their father's hunched figure on the long journey home.

A thin crescent moon was rising by the time they got back to the village. Mama's eyes lit up as they came through the door, but they saw her joy fade as she looked in vain for Dorota to follow them in.

Papa laid the coins on the table, and they glowed red in the light from the fire.

Chapter 4

L EO HEARD HIS SISTER MARIA WHISPER TO THE THREE-YEAR-OLD twins, Frederyk and Helena, that they mustn't talk about Dorota, but no one else mentioned her name. He knew that everyone was thinking about her, though—especially Mama, who kept one of Dorota's headscarves entwined around the belt of her skirt.

Papa hardly spoke for a week and everyone moved around him carefully, fearful of sparking his hurt into anger. In the evenings, he sat next to the fire weaving a pair of birch-bark sandals. When he finished them, he placed them next to the fireplace, and there they stayed, waiting for the day Dorota would come home.

A thaw set in, and the village began to emerge from the whiteness. Soon the track and courtyard were a muddy mess, and even the clay floor inside the house started to darken and sweat. But the sun felt good on the face, and it took the chill out of the wind. Spring was on the way.

The ponds on the river meadows melted and Alexsy, who was a patient and clever trapper, wove a funnel out of wild vetches and caught some large eels with it. Two went straight into the stewpot, and he nailed the rest to stakes and smoked them over a fire so they wouldn't spoil. He started taking Stefan and Maria with him and taught them how to catch crayfish, and one day Stefan came home proudly holding a carp they had caught.

Then, to complete the sense of hope, the storks came back to their pole. Jozef was thrilled and, now that the chickens and geese were gone, he watched the storks instead and gave everyone detailed reports of their comings and goings. Even the priest knew of Jozef's interest, and one Sunday as the family was leaving church, he bent down to the little boy and asked, "So, how are your storks doing today, young man?"

Jozef colored, coughed nervously, and said, "They're not mine— they're Leo's. He saw them first. They came because of him."

"Quite so, quite so," the priest said, smiling. Then he stood up and took Papa's arm. "A word?"

Papa nodded and gestured the family to move away. They stood at the edge of the churchyard and watched while the two men talked.

It was later in the afternoon that Papa revealed what had been said.

"It seems there might be the chance of work for you," he said to Leo as the two of them were carrying wood back from the forest.

Leo's heart skipped. Work. Where? Who for? A farmer or a craftsman? It would be hard to leave home. But he would do anything to help the family. Perhaps it would be in Nakel. Perhaps he would see Dorota.

He looked sideways at Papa but didn't ask. Let Papa take his time.

"The priest told me that there's been an accident up at the Manor. One of the herdsmen got his leg crushed. They're looking for someone to help out until he's better."

Leo felt as if the breath had been sucked out of him. The Manor. Anywhere but there. Borys and his rope. Wolfgang, with his cruel sneers.

There was a long silence. Leo looked at Papa. There was no escape. Papa moved his head slightly in a silent question.

It will be all right, Leo told himself. It will be all right.

And to Papa's silent question, he spoke the answer. "Yes."

Chapter 5

As HE WALKED UP THE LONG DRIVE TO THE MANOR, LEO TOUCHED the pocket of his waistcoat. Inside were the stork feather Jozef had given him for luck, and the scrap of paper Mama had taken down from her collection of holy images on the cottage wall.

"If I can't look after you, I know the Holy Mother will," she had said, folding the drawing of the Virgin Mary. As she had made the last fold, one of her tears had fallen onto the paper. That precious scrap of paper, the stork feather, and his bark sandals wrapped in his spare sacking shirt were all the belongings Leo had brought from home.

He rounded a corner, and there, at the end of the line of bare chestnut trees, was the Manor. A chill ran across Leo's shoulders, but he kept walking. Home was only a three hours' walk away. Perhaps the Baron would let him go home sometimes. He would take his earnings with him and proudly hand them over to Papa.

He repeated to himself the phrase that Papa had given him to say: "I have come to see the Baron, please."

"Speak only to the Baron," Papa had told him. "He will remember the good work you did last year. He may be a Prussian but he's an honest man and fair. Other landlords would have driven us off the farm for the debts we owe, but not him."

"I have come to see the Baron, please," Leo repeated as he walked under the arch and into the courtyard of the Manor. Then he stopped, and his heart jerked with fear.

Wolfgang and Borys were there, sitting on their horses.

Leo's first instinct was to duck out of sight, but he forced himself to walk forward across the courtyard. Borys saw him coming and nodded to Wolfgang, who glanced around briefly and then went on talking.

Leo arrived next to them and stood there, heart pounding—not daring to interrupt as Wolfgang talked to Borys about some work that needed to be done on the water mill.

Finally, Wolfgang turned and looked down at Leo.

"Well, well, the debtor's son," he sneered. "I thought there was a bad smell. What do you want?"

"I have come to see the Baron, please."

"My father is not here. He's been called away to Berlin."

"When will he back, please?"

"Back?" Wolfgang snapped. "Don't you know anything, damn you? My father's a general, yes? And there's a war looming with France, yes? So he'll be back when the crisis is over or when the war is won. Until then, I am the man of the house. So what have you come for?"

"The priest told us that one of your herdsmen is injured."

"So?"

"I thought—" Leo's throat choked with shyness and embarrassment, and he had to cough before he could force the rest of the words out, "—you could hire me."

Wolfgang burst into raucous laughter, and his horse skittered sideways into Leo, knocking him off balance. He fell to the ground but was up again in a flash, scrambling out of the way of the horse's hooves.

"What do you think, Borys?" Wolfgang said when they both stopped laughing. "Do we need a puny, smelly pup on the estate?"

Borys held his nose in mock disgust and shook his head.

"So there's your answer. No." Wolfgang laughed. "Now get back to your filthy kennel."

Wolfgang dug his heels into his horse's flanks and cantered across the courtyard and out through the archway, followed by Borys.

Leo trudged back down the drive, lost in a turmoil of emotions. He was disappointed that he hadn't been hired, because he knew how much the money would have helped the family. And it was going to be hard telling Papa. But at least he wouldn't have to face Wolfgang's insults and cruelty.

"Leo! Leo!"

He looked up and saw old Gregory coming across the field, followed by his herd of cows. He had been Leo's only friend last year, always ready with an encouraging word of praise or a funny story to cheer him up when he felt low.

As Gregory grew closer, Leo could see that he had aged since last harvest time. His hair was whiter and his ruddy complexion was crisscrossed with deep creases, but his eyes were still blue and filled with kindness.

"Leo, my little smiling friend!" Gregory said, giving him a hug and a slap on the back. "What are you doing here?"

Leo explained what had happened.

"Wolfgang! He's got the devil in his heart, that one," Gregory muttered. "And Borys encourages him in his wildness. His mother can't control him and, with the Baron away, there's no one to keep him in check. You know that injured herdsman? The Baron would have called a doctor or a wise woman to treat him. Not Wolfgang—he coldly sent the lad back to his village. Now the gangrene's set in, and he's likely to die."

"All I want is work," Leo said. "You know how hard I can work."

"It's an unhappy country where willing workers are shunned.

Look at me—years of service, but they could put me out tomorrow. I should have followed my brother to America. Left to find his fortune, didn't he? And like a fool, I stayed."

"And did he?" Leo asked. "Find his fortune?"

"I only heard from him once. He got someone to write a letter for him, and I got the priest to read it to me. He was in Minnesota. There's a name! I remember it well—the priest had such a job getting his tongue 'round the saying of it. Minn-e-sota! That was long ago. So he will be rich now, I'm sure. Rich. Free. His own master in America. And me, no better than a serf."

Gregory sighed and gently patted the rump of one of his beloved cows as she moved past him, her full udder swinging. "Well, I'd better get this lot milked. God go with you, little smiler."

He gave Leo a hug and went off toward the milking barn, encouraging the cows with gentle words as they ambled slowly across the field.

Leo reached the end of the drive and started on the long way home. He'd been walking for about ten minutes and was nearing the river when he heard a feeble bleating from the ditch at the side of the track. He parted some nettles and found two tiny lambs lying there. Their wool was wet from where they had stumbled through the water in the ditch, and they were shivering pitifully.

He stood up and looked across the fields. The nearest sheep were a long way away, grazing on a hillside. Something must have happened—either the mother had died, or she had simply abandoned these two. Either way, no other ewe would accept them. The only way they could be saved would be to hand-rear them.

For a moment he thought of taking them back to the Manor and giving them to Gregory, but then he made up his mind. Two abandoned lambs would never be missed from the Baron's huge flock. Two abandoned lambs would mean so much to the family's small flock of six. They would need a lot of looking after, but Jozef was the one for that. He would care for them and feed them. They would grow strong.

He glanced around quickly, bent down, picked up the wet little bundles, and tucked them inside his waistcoat. The lambs bleated and struggled briefly then, as he began to walk and his body heat warmed them, they settled down. He looked at the tubby shape of his waistcoat and smiled as he imagined making Jozef guess what was in there. And he could hear the cries of delight from little Helena and Frederyk when he showed them the tiny lambs.

He had only been walking for about five minutes when he heard hoofbeats from ahead. They were coming from the direction of the river—from the direction of the water mill.

He stood still in horror as two riders swept out of the trees and galloped along the track toward him.

It was Wolfgang and Borys.

Chapter 6

WOLFGANG AND BORYS STOPPED CLOSE TO LEO. THEY LOOKED at each other with sly smiles and then began circling him on their horses.

"What have you got there?" Wolfgang asked, pointing to the bulge in Leo's waistcoat.

"I found them," he said.

"Found what?" Borys asked.

"Lambs. They've been abandoned."

"Oh, poor little abandoned lambikins," Wolfgang said in a babyish voice.

"Show!" Borys ordered.

Leo pulled the lambs from his waistcoat and held them up, turning to keep pace with the circling horses.

"Well, well, Borys, I do believe we've caught a thief," Wolfgang said with an excited giggle.

"They're abandoned," Leo said. "No ewe would accept them. They would have to be reared by hand."

"Ah, so you were going to rear them? You were going to be their mommy!" Wolfgang said, stopping his horse directly in front of him. "Is that it?"

Leo nodded and glanced over his shoulder at Borys, who had stopped his horse and was climbing down.

"My lambs?" Wolfgang roared. "You were taking my lambs?

Give them to me."

Leo held the tiny lambs up. Wolfgang reached down and snatched them—one by the scruff of its neck, and the other by its leg. The lambs bleated. He looked at them for a moment, and then carelessly flung them over his shoulder. They flew high through the air, landed in a crumpled heap on the track, and lay still.

"You're a thief. A common thief!" Wolfgang said coldly. "Take him."

Shame and guilt overwhelmed Leo, and he meekly held out his hands while Borys tied his wrists and attached the rope to the pommel of his saddle.

Wolfgang and Borys kicked their horses into a trot and Leo ran behind them, terrified that he would fall and be dragged along the ground by the rope. When they finally reached the Manor and stopped in front of one of the hay barns, he fell to his knees, desperately sucking air into his burning lungs.

Borys jerked him upright by his hair, untied the rope, pulled him to the barn, and threw him inside. Leo collapsed on the floor and heard the bar being secured across the door. He crawled to the pile of hay in the corner and lay there, trembling with exhaustion and fear.

If only he hadn't heard the bleating of those lambs. If only he had left them there to die.

But he had heard them. And he had taken them. He had broken the law. And now he was in the hands of Wolfgang and Borys.

What would they do to him? There would be no mercy from Wolfgang. He loved having power over people. It thrilled him to ride around the estate and see how the workers bowed their heads because they were scared of him.

And he loved having the power of life and death over animals. Look how he had killed those lambs. That was typical of him. Last year, he had ridden around the pasture chasing a cow until he had driven the poor creature crazy with fright. It had fallen into a pit and broken a leg, and he had laughed as he drew his pistol and shot it in the head. Gregory had told him that he'd once seen Wolfgang flog a horse so badly it had been blinded and had to be destroyed.

He was mad and vicious. And now that his father wasn't here to stop him, he could treat men almost as badly as he treated animals.

Leo's fears grew with each passing hour, and when he heard voices outside the barn he held his breath. Was it them? The voices went away, and he tried to calm himself.

Even Wolfgang couldn't keep him locked up here forever. He'd have to let him out soon. Perhaps he was just trying to scare him. But scaring him wouldn't be enough for Wolfgang. He would want more. Perhaps he would send for the police or the Mayor. Even if Leo tried to explain exactly what had happened, they would only see it one way—he had tried to steal the lambs. He was a thief.

The very word made him dizzy with panic, and he forced himself to think of other things. Home.

Mama. How she would worry if she could see him now. How he longed to feel her comforting arms around him. And Papa, so strong and reliable. What would Papa say? "You can endure."

Yes, he could endure. Like poor Dorota was enduring in that tavern. Like Jozef endured when his chest was bad and he struggled to breathe. So many times, Leo had seen the terror in his little brother's eyes as he gasped for a breath but, when that breath finally came, he always smiled as if to apologize for the fear he had shown. If Jozef could endure that and survive, then Leo could face anything Wolfgang did to him.

A long time passed, and then there was the sound of the bar being lifted from the door. Late afternoon sunshine flooded in, blinding him. A shadow fell across him, and he could see the silhouette of Borys standing in the barn doorway.

"You. This way," Borys barked, and Leo followed him out, around the hay barn and along the side of the Manor House.

Borys was carrying the thick cane that was used to flog wrongdoers, and by the time they turned the corner and passed under the arch into the courtyard, Leo's heart was pounding with terror. Last year, he had seen one of the ploughmen flogged for some mistake he had made. Borys had given him fifteen terrible strokes and the man had cried out in agony.

The punishment bench was standing on the gravel in the middle of the courtyard. The workers from the estate were all there, arranged in a semicircle around the bench to witness the punishment. He saw Gregory and Kassia, the pretty young kitchen maid who had been so friendly and kind to him last year. They both lowered their eyes as if they couldn't bear to watch.

Numbly, Leo walked toward the punishment bench and stopped next to it. Wolfgang was standing close by, his eyes alight with excitement.

Borys stepped forward and addressed the workers. "This boy is a thief. For this offense, he will receive eight strokes of the cane."

Borys pulled Leo's waistcoat off and then tapped the side of the bench with the cane, signaling him to lie down.

What could he do? Papa had told him that the wind always blows in the face of the poor. This was it—that cruel wind. This was the power that could do whatever it pleased. He was alone and defeated.

He lay down on the bench.

He mustn't cry out. Mustn't beg. He must close his mind. Think of home. Think of Jozef and the courage he showed when his lungs ached and he could barely breathe.

"Master," Borys said, and Leo turned his head. The overseer was handing the cane to Wolfgang.

"No! Not him!" Leo shouted, starting to get up.

Borys's hand thumped into his back, pinning him to the bench.

"Gregory! Marek! Grab his arms and legs!" Borys ordered, and the two men stepped forward. "Hold him tight."

The men seized him and he twisted and writhed, trying to break their grip. Gregory was holding his wrists, and he leaned forward and whispered, "Take it, little one—a boy cannot hit as hard as Borys."

The words made sense, but still Leo fought. Then Gregory whispered again, "He thinks you're afraid."

At once, he stopped struggling. He looked up at Gregory, and the old man pursed his eyebrows in encouragement.

There was a long pause, and then he heard the whistle of the cane and felt a thud on his buttocks. For a moment, the line of stinging pain seemed to stay on the surface of his skin, but then it burned deep into his flesh. There was another long pause, and then came a second cut of the cane. Then a third. He fought to stay still and not cry out.

There was an even longer pause before the fourth blow hit the back of his thighs, making his legs jerk in shock and nearly breaking Marek's grip on his ankles.

The fifth blow hit him across his back, just below his shoulder blades. Wolfgang was deliberately spreading the pain all over his body. The sixth stroke caught him slightly lower down, whipping across his spine and onto the right side of his back, while the tip of the cane sprang around and lashed at his ribs. He could stay silent no longer, and he gasped and groaned. The seventh cut landed in almost the same place, again catching his ribs. Then the eighth stroke sliced across his buttocks again and he whimpered with pain.

"It's over," Gregory whispered, and gave Leo's wrists a gentle squeeze before letting go.

Slowly, Leo rolled off the bench and stood up. The movement increased the pain, and he wobbled slightly as he turned around to face the line of workers. Their faces were grim.

"Now, get on your knees," Wolfgang said. "Kiss my feet and beg my forgiveness."

No. He was in pain from the beating. He had taken the punishment, but he would not be broken. He would not kneel to this boy.

"I will not," he said. His voice trembled slightly, but no one could doubt his determination and there was a murmur from the workers.

Wolfgang glanced at them, and Leo saw the nervous look that flashed across his face.

"You dog!" Wolfgang said. "How dare you disobey your master! Get on your knees!"

Leo shook his head.

"On your knees, I said!"

Wolfgang lifted the cane and struck him across the side of the face.

The pain burned from his jaw to his ear but Leo refused the temptation to reach up and rub it.

"You're thieving scum," Wolfgang hissed. "And you come from a family of scum. A lazy father who lives in debt. A mother who whelps children like a bitch whelps puppies. How many of you are there now? Twenty? Answer me!"

"Eight."

"Eight? I wonder how many of the village men your mother slept with to have so many children."

"Stop it!" Leo said, and a smirk flashed across Wolfgang's face.

"What did you say? Stop? Who do you think you are? You

dress in rags, you stink like a pig, yet you dare to give me orders? Well, I'll teach you some manners. I'll teach you to show respect to your betters."

Wolfgang raised the cane again and Leo flew at him. His fist hit Wolfgang in the mouth, cutting his lip. The second blow smashed into his nose, sending him staggering backward and onto the ground. Leo dove on top of him, punching wildly at Wolfgang's chest and face.

Then hands grabbed him and hauled him up. He turned to see who it was and a crunching blow hit him on the side of his head. His legs crumpled. There was another stunning blow, and he was gone.

Chapter 7

LEO WOKE AND DIDN'T KNOW WHERE HE WAS. IT WAS DARK. HE was facedown on the floor, with straw under him. He must be in the barn. He ached—everywhere. His head was throbbing and the side of his face felt swollen. He rolled over onto his back, and the pain made him groan. His stomach heaved and he turned his head and vomited a sour liquid. He turned on his front again, and it all came back to him. The flogging. The fight.

He forced himself to his feet and, despite the stabs of pain in his ribs and his legs, he limped through the darkness until he came to the wall. He felt his way along to the doors and pushed on them. They were shut and barred.

He moved back and lay down again. He was a prisoner. What were they going to do with him? His heart clenched with fear and he tried to drive the thoughts away by concentrating on his aching body. As long as he lay still, the only sharp pain was the throbbing in his head. All the rest was just a dull soreness.

Rain began to fall. He lost all sense of time and fell into a kind of trance as he listened to the pattering on the roof and the splattering on the ground outside the door. Then, suddenly, all his senses were startled alive by another noise in the darkness—here, in the barn. An animal?

"Leo?" came a hoarse whisper. "Leo, it's me—Gregory."

"Gregory," he said softly, and winced as he got up onto his knees.

There was a rustling in the straw, and he sensed Gregory near him. He reached out and touched the old herdsman's leg.

"Ah, there you are," Gregory breathed, squatting down and putting his hand on Leo's shoulder.

"How did you get in?"

"There are some loose boards at the back. I loosened them a bit more. I couldn't just leave you to your fate."

"Why?" Leo asked, a chill sweeping up his back.

"Why? Mother of God, you defied a nobleman's son, child. You punched him, cut his lip, bloodied his nose. If we hadn't all been standing there, I swear Borys and Wolfgang would have beaten and kicked you to death on the spot. And the law would have taken their side."

"What are they going to do?"

"They've sent for the mayor from Exin, and he'll be here in the morning. There'll be no trial. Wolfgang will only need to tell him what happened, and you will be found guilty. There will be another flogging, and you will be thrown into the jail in Wirsitz for a year, perhaps more."

"A year?" Leo gasped.

"The nobles will demand it—they crush rebellion without mercy. And jail can kill grown men, Leo, let alone a child like you. There are diseases. Poor food. Filthy water. Punishments. And some prisoners, no better than godless beasts, who will do evil things to a lad."

There was a long terrible pause with only the sound of the falling rain.

"What can I do?" Leo asked.

"I will show you the loose boards, and you must go."

"Home?"

"No! No! Not if you love your family. They would be accused of sheltering a criminal, and Wolfgang would use it as an excuse to drive them off his land. But if they search and don't find you there, he can do nothing."

"But where will I go?"

"I can't tell you, little one. But far away. And leave no trace for them to follow. Wolfgang wants revenge, and he will not give up easily."

A sudden gust of wind hammered the rain against the barn.

"Come," Gregory whispered. He took Leo's arm and led him through the darkness to the back of the barn. "Wait here, and I'll go and check that there's no one around."

Leo's legs were weak and his whole body throbbed with pain. He leaned against the wall, and his mind whirled in confusion. Another beating? Jail? Run away? Leave home?

Only yesterday morning, his life had been so good. Even when he had been turned down for work, he had still had a home to go to. Parents who loved him. A family to welcome him. But now all that was gone—all swept away by a moment of madness. He should have kneeled and kissed Wolfgang's feet. He should have closed his ears to the insults, and he would be home by now. But it was too late. What was done was done, and it couldn't be undone.

And now what?

Jail? It was true what Gregory said—he could die in there. He had heard about the jail in Wirsitz. Prisoners were beaten and chained to the wall, sometimes for days. The cells were tiny, and men were crowded together, lying in their own filth and covered with lice. And if he managed to survive, what kind of life would he come back to? He would carry the name "criminal" forever, and his family would suffer the shame.

But leave home? Never to see Papa and Mama again? Never to laugh and play with his brothers and sisters again? To be out in the world, alone, with no one to care for him. He couldn't. He couldn't.

But if he went home, he would bring disaster to them. The farm would be taken. They would be homeless and starving. He would rather die than let that happen.

There was no choice. He would have to go. The very thought of it brought stinging tears to his eyes and he could feel sobs rising in his chest. At any moment, it would overwhelm him and he would fall to the ground in defeat.

Endure, Papa always said. But this? It was too hard. He couldn't endure this torture. He shook his head in the dark, and the tears splashed down his face.

"No, no tears," he told himself, and he ran his hand over his face to wipe them away. "It will be all right. It will be all right." But hot tears continued to trickle down his cheeks.

"Leo," came Gregory's whisper in the darkness. "Through here."

Somehow he found the strength to move. He slipped between the loose boards and out into the rainy night.

The two guard dogs chained under the archway started to growl as they approached, but Gregory spoke quietly to them and they settled down again.

"There are three hours before daylight," Gregory said as they stood on the drive. "And with this rain, the mayor won't arrive until midmorning. They will waste time trying to find how you escaped. Then more time searching the grounds. With any luck, you will have six or seven hours' start on them."

Leo threw his arms around Gregory's waist and clung on, almost as if the old man could perform a miracle and make this misery stop. But after a moment, Gregory gently pushed him away.

"It's a wild road you'll have to walk, my child. Wild and dangerous. But God will be with you." He made the sign of the cross on Leo's forehead and kissed the top of his head. "Ah, you are so like my brother. Same smile. Same good heart. You will be free and lucky like him. I know it. Now go, quickly—go."

Leo turned and began to run down the drive—slowly and painfully at first, but gathering strength as the movement eased the pain in his muscles. The rain cascaded down his face, mixing with his tears.

Chapter 8

IN THE RAINY NIGHT, LEO TOOK THE ONLY ROAD HE KNEW—THE one that led back to his village.

It was still dark when he got home, and he squatted in the shelter of the birch trees on the sandy bank and watched the first faint light of day gradually pick out the details of his family's cabin below. The dark logs of the walls, the door, the window, and, a short time later, a red glow from the interior as Mama, always the first to get up in the morning, put wood on the fire. He glimpsed movements inside and he pictured the activities as everyone got out of bed and began the routines of the day.

The front door opened and Stefan came out, carrying the chamber pot. He carefully emptied its contents into the ditch by the side of the track and then looked up and scanned the sky intently. When he got back inside, Papa would ask him for a prediction of the day's weather. Papa was expert at judging the weather and he loved teaching the skill to his children. Leo quickly checked the sky and decided that the rain would stop soon. The low cloud cover would burn away and it would be a fine day.

A fine day for the mayor of Exin to send out a search party for him. He should be miles away, not lingering here. This was the first place they would look. But he couldn't leave without seeing his family one last time.

Stefan went inside and closed the door. There was no movement in the house now, and Leo's stomach grumbled as he imagined the breakfast they were all eating—each a chunk of rye bread and a bowl of steaming cabbage soup. Perhaps Mama would add some bacon or mutton fat to enrich it, and the golden globules would be shining on the surface of the soup.

Papa was the first to emerge after breakfast, and Leo's heart swelled as he watched him. He stood in the middle of the court-yard and swung his arms to stretch the muscles in his shoulders, then he walked into the little barn and emerged with a hoe and a rake. He must be going down to the field to tend the spring flax that he had sown just after the snow. He crossed the farm yard and came out onto the track.

His heart beating fast, Leo crept to the edge of the bank and peered down as Papa walked away—that graying hair and that broad back, slightly stooped, as though it was weighed down with worries.

Leo longed to call out to him, longed to run down there, tell him the whole story, and ask him for advice. But he knew what would happen. Papa would never let one of his children take to the road alone. He would order him to stay. Then there would be Mama—with tears in her eyes, holding his face in her hands while she whispered how much she loved him and then begged him to stay. It would be impossible to resist. He would stay, and Wolfgang and Borys would find him there. They would drive the family off the farm, and it would be all his fault.

No, he had to go.

Leo closed his eyes and made a vow. One day, he would earn enough money to make life better for everyone. He would make everything right. He would buy the best fields and the best animals for Papa, and a horse to help plow the fields. There would be fine clothes for Mama, and someone to help her in the house. And food for everyone.

The door of the house banged and Stefan dashed out and across the courtyard. He bounded along the track and skidded to a halt next to Papa, who handed him the rake then looked up at the sky. Stefan anxiously followed his gaze and then his eager face broke into a smile as Papa said something—his weather forecast must have been correct. They turned and headed down the track. Leo watched until they were gone.

A few minutes later, Alexsy and Jozef came out of the house and crossed the yard to the sheep pen. Alexsy opened the gate, and together they drove the five sheep out of the pen and across the yard. How grown up Alexsy looked. How like Papa he was becoming—the strength in the arms, the broadness of his hands, and the solid way he stood, as though he were part of the land. Alexsy would never leave this place. He would work alongside Papa, helping him and—one day—taking over for him.

Leo got up and ran along the bank, through the birch trees to a place above the little path where he could watch his brothers go by. The sheep ambled into view, followed by Alexsy and Jozef. The little boy's spindly legs looked almost too frail to carry him, and pain squeezed Leo's heart. How could he leave here? Leave his family? Leave Jozef, perhaps never to see him again?

The two boys stopped directly below him.

"Are you sure you want to come, Jo?" Leo heard Alexsy ask. "You can stay at home and watch the storks if you want."

"I want to come with you," Jozef said.

Alexsy smiled and ruffled his little brother's hair.

"All right," he said. "I'm a bit hot, though. Can you wear my scarf for me?"

Jozef nodded, and Alexsy tenderly wrapped the scarf around his brother's neck and tucked it into his waistcoat. They continued up the path toward the grazing ground.

Leo returned to his spot overlooking the house just in time to see Mama. She was heading away across the field in the direction of the river. Maria was by her side and they were both carrying clothes. The twins were toddling along behind them—Frederyk kept racing ahead of Helena, but he fell over so often that she always caught up with him. They would play by the river while Mama and Maria knelt on the bank, washing the clothes.

Almost as if she sensed Leo's presence, Mama suddenly stopped and turned around. She bundled the clothes under one arm and lifted her free hand to shield her eyes as she peered in his direction. He knew she wouldn't be able to see him, hidden behind the bush, but he could see her clearly—her broad red face, circled by her headscarf, and the knuckles of her hands, knobbly and swollen from the arthritis that plagued her.

She lowered her hand and briefly touched her belly. Was the baby beginning to move already, that brother or sister he wouldn't see, perhaps for years? Then Mama turned away from him and hurried to catch up with Maria and the twins. When they reached the steep dip that led down to the river, Mama took Helena's hand. A few seconds later, they were all gone, hidden from his sight.

Leo scrambled down the bank and ran across the path to the house. He opened the door and looked in. It was his home but he already felt like a stranger there. He stared hard at everything, trying to fix a picture in his mind for the future, for those lonely times when he knew he would want to remember every detail of it.

Then he closed the door.

There was one last person to see.

Chapter 9

HE PEERED THROUGH THE FRONT WINDOW OF THE TAVERN AND saw Dorota serving the customers but he didn't dare go in. If Borys or the mayor of Exin found out he'd been in Nakel, they might guess the direction he was planning to take. So he crept around the back of the building and waited at the open kitchen door, his body aching and his heart filled with doubt.

Two small pigs were squealing and grunting as they competed with each other for the rubbish in the alleyway. He watched them squabble until he heard someone come into the kitchen. He peeked through the door and saw Dorota carrying a tray piled with plates and glasses. She put the tray on the table and then looked up and saw him.

For a brief instant, she stared in puzzled surprise. Then she rushed to the doorway and threw her arms around him, kissing his cheek and saying his name over and over.

"Stop it—people will think I'm your boyfriend!" he joked, and Dorota laughed and planted another kiss on his other cheek, right where Wolfgang had struck him. He winced, and she stepped back and noticed the bruise.

"What's happened?" she whispered, gently running a finger across his face, tracing the line of swelling.

He began to tell his story, and tears filled her eyes as she listened.

"Go away?" she said when he finished.

"I've got to. If I go home, they'll catch me. They'll send me to jail, and Wolfgang will drive us off the farm. But if I go away, he won't be able to do anything."

"You can't go! You can't," she said. "What will I do without you, Leo?"

"You'll manage."

"But where will you go? What will you do?"

"I don't know."

"Where will you sleep? How will you eat?"

"I don't know." He shook his head, and suddenly it all seemed impossible. "Oh, Dorota, I'm so scared."

She scanned his face anxiously and saw his fear.

"No, no. Don't be scared," she said, putting her arms around him. "You'll be all right. You're strong."

"I'm not."

"Yes, you are. You're my big brother—the one who always looked after me and called me your little pet. You're strong enough to do anything." Her voice trembled, and she pulled him close and began to sob.

"Shhh. Don't, Dorota, don't," he whispered. How many times had they held on to each other like this, giving each other comfort and courage? "I'll make money. I'll send it home to Papa and you won't have to work in this place. I'll go to America and—"

"America?" Dorota gasped, pulling away from him in shock. "So far?"

"Gregory's brother went there and made his fortune. I can too. I'll do it. I swear. And I'll send the money home, and Papa can buy more fields, better land, and more animals, and there'll be food for everyone."

"Oh, Leo, I'll be so alone without you. No one to make me laugh the way you do. No one to share my secrets with. No one."

"Dorota!" screeched a woman's voice from inside the tavern.

"I'm coming," she called.

"What's she like?"

Dorota shrugged, and that little movement told Leo everything. They had shared so much together, and knew each other so well. Again, he felt the rush of desire to help. He would make things better for her too. He would.

"I've got to go," she said.

"Dorota, you must get word to Papa and Mama. Tell them I'm all right. Tell them I love them. And that I'm sorry. And tell them that I'll come back one day. Can you do that?"

"I'll find a way," she said, taking his hand and kissing it. "Don't forget me, promise?"

"How could I? Never," he swore. "Never. You're my little pet, remember? And you always will be. I'll make money. I'll make money and you'll be able to go home—I promise."

She pulled him to her and hugged him.

"Dorota!" screamed that voice again.

"Good-bye," she whispered. She broke away from him and darted into the tavern.

Leo ran down the alley, past the back of the church, and away toward the bridge. He scrambled down the steep bank by the side of the bridge and onto the towpath.

The Bromberg Canal lay before him, its waters blue from the reflection of the clear sky. The straight banks stretched away, narrowing to a far distant point on the horizon as if to remind him of the length of the journey ahead.

He took one step forward and then stopped, suddenly overwhelmed by what he was doing. This was it—the road away from everything he knew. The road from home.

He could turn back.

No, it would be all right. It would be all right.

He took one step, then another, and then another.

PART TWO

The Road

Chapter 10

Leo kept looking back toward Nakel, seeing the houses become smaller and smaller until, at last, the town disappeared from view and he couldn't even make out the smoke rising from the chimneys.

For nearly an hour he was alone on the towpath but then he saw a barge in the distance. He scampered up the embankment and hid behind the bushes until it passed. Almost immediately another barge appeared, and then another, so he decided to go down into the woods on the other side of the embankment. There was no path down there, and he had to force his way through bushes and brambles. Thorns and branches scratched him, and clumps of impenetrable undergrowth drove him farther and farther off course until he finally lost sight of the embankment.

One of his birch sandals came off and he stopped, waist high in brambles, and felt around with his foot until he found it and slipped it back on. He took another couple of steps and then lost the sandal again. He twisted around, searching for it, and the brambles jabbed and stabbed him. By the time he found the sandal, clouds of flies were buzzing around him as if they were drawn to the blood oozing from his scratches. He pushed on for a bit longer and then gave up and struggled back the way he'd come.

Suddenly all the problems crashed in on him.

What was he doing? Going to America. America? He didn't

even know where it was. Across the sea, they said. But where was the sea? How far away? It was a stupid plan. How could he get to America alone? He had no money, no possessions, and no one to help him. It was impossible.

He stood in the gloomy woods, feeling hopeless and defeated. He couldn't go on. He couldn't go home. He couldn't do anything.

Then he remembered the promises he had made to himself, and the things he'd said to Dorota. He had sworn to help the family. He couldn't let them down. He couldn't give up so soon. He couldn't.

He angrily brushed away the flies and pushed his way back through the bushes toward the canal. He might not know where the sea was, but he knew the canal went to Bromberg. And Bromberg was a big town. He would find work there. He would earn money. He would find out where the sea was. He would go there, get on a boat, and go to America. It could be done. He would do it.

He burst out of the bushes and climbed up the embankment. There was the canal again, a true and straight line showing him the way to go.

For the next couple of hours, he walked slowly, watching the water change color as the sky faded from the deep blue of the afternoon to the pink of early evening. Swallows skimmed low over the canal, chasing insects. Fish rose, sending lazy circles rippling out across the surface. Then, as the light drained from the sky, bats flitted above and around him.

The chill of dew started to drop on his shoulders, and he was about to go down into the woods to look for shelter for the night when he saw a small triangle of flame in the darkness ahead. He crept along the embankment toward its flicker. A barge was tied up to the bank, and the bargeman was sitting next to his fire on the towpath. A big horse was grazing on the grass nearby.

The man leaned forward and lifted the lid from the pot hanging over the fire. A tempting smell rose up, and Leo's mouth watered as he watched the man spoon the food onto a metal plate and begin to eat. Was there enough for two? Would he share? Leo gazed at the man in the flickering light, trying to gauge his character. He was old. His long hair and big, droopy moustache were gray, and the lines on his face were deep and shadowy. His body was restless—his legs jiggled and his hand trembled as he shoveled the food into his mouth. Perhaps he was nervous or he had an illness that gave him tics, but there was something edgy and dangerous about all that fidgety movement.

The food smelled wonderful, though, and Leo was so hungry that he ignored the warning signs and slowly made his way down the embankment to the towpath. The horse saw him first and lifted its head and shuffled nervously, making the bargeman look up. Leo stopped and spread his hands out wide to show that he wasn't a threat. The old man squinted at him for a long time, and then went back to wolfing down his meal. Leo took a few steps toward the fire and then stopped again, watching as the man used a piece of bread to mop up the juice on his plate.

"Open the larder, and the dogs come sniffing around," the man said, popping the piece of bread in his mouth. His voice was strange—high-pitched and squeaky, as if he had to squeeze the words out. "You'll be trying to scrounge some food."

"I'll work for it," Leo said.

"Ha! Work for it!" the man cackled. "A scrawny runt like you? Pull my barge, will you? I've got a horse for that. And I'm all the crew I need. I don't need anybody."

The delicious smell from the pot was even stronger down here and, for a moment, Leo thought about begging for some food, but then he turned away and headed back toward the dark embankment. He scrambled up to the top and lay down under a tree. The man might be unfriendly, but that fire was reassuring in the dark night—better to sleep here than alone in the woods.

The man rinsed his plate in the canal and then took a bottle from the deck of the barge. He took a couple of gulps and lifted his head to drain the last few drops. Then, he looked at the empty bottle and threw it into the canal with a curse. He slumped down next to the fire, put his hands on either side of his head, and rocked backward and forward as if trying to ease a painful headache. After a minute, he stopped and looked up toward Leo.

"Hey, you! You up there!" he shouted. "I know you're there. You can do something for me."

Leo lay still.

"There's food for you. Look," the man said, struggling to his feet and holding up the pot. "You can have what's left. Bread too."

"What do I have to do?" Leo called.

"Guard my barge and horse while I go to the tavern. It's not far. By the time you eat your fill, I'll be back. What d'you say?"

The lure of the food was too great, and Leo got up and ran down to the towpath.

"It's just the scrapings, but you can soak up the juices with this," the man said, holding out a big chunk of bread. "That'll stop your belly growling."

Leo sat down and lifted the lid of the pot. There wasn't much stew left—a few flakes of fish and some shreds of cabbage—but there was plenty of gravy, and he was about to dip the bread in it when he heard a clinking noise. He looked around and saw the man walking toward him with an ax in his hand. He scuttled back in terror, desperately trying to get to his feet.

The man stopped. A brief, mocking smile raised his lips, then disappeared.

"If I wanted to kill you, I wouldn't use an ax," he said. "It's for you. Protection, in case anyone takes a mind to steal my horse or the cargo."

"Is your cargo valuable?" Leo asked as he stood up and took the ax.

"People steal first and check what it's worth later. See this?" he lifted his chin and pointed to a scar that ran across his throat. "Got it fifteen years ago on the banks of the Oder. Bandits came out of the forest. They slit my windpipe and then looked at my cargo. Fifteen geese and a calf. They didn't care. Better than nothing. They made off with the geese and the calf, and left me to croak. But I didn't—see? I stuck a rag in the hole in my throat, made it into town, and got myself sewed up. Right as rain— except my voice sounds like a strangled weasel. Leastways, that's what my wife said before she went running back to her mother."

He spat toward the fire, and Leo hoped it hadn't fallen into the pot.

"So—if anyone turns up," the man went on, "you show him that ax and look as if you're ready to stave his brains in with it. Right?"

Leo nodded and watched as the man walked out of the firelight and disappeared into the night. Soon his footsteps faded and Leo sat down, cradling the ax across his knees and feeling alone and scared.

Chapter 11

A SPARK EXPLODED IN THE FIRE, AND A SHIVER RAN DOWN Leo's back as he imagined bandits creeping out of the woods to slit his throat. The darkness felt full of menace, and he strained his eyes and ears to detect danger until hunger finally overcame his fear. He put the ax down and began to eat.

By the time he had wiped the pot clean and finished the last crumb of bread, his eyes felt heavy but he didn't dare lie down and sleep. The horse snorted and stamped its heavy hooves as if it was restless, so Leo got up and went over to it. It was a huge creature, with a big muscular back and shoulders from pulling the barge, but it shied away timidly and went to the limit of its tether as Leo approached.

"Whoa!" he said gently, stopping still and letting the horse get used to him. "Shhh! There's a good boy." He crossed to the embankment, pulled some long grass, and held it out. "Come on, then."

He waited until the horse finally shuffled forward, its eyes alert and its head swaying from side to side. It took the grass, and as it munched, Leo slid his hand up onto its muzzle and rubbed the soft skin between its nostrils. Twice, it jerked its head upward, rejecting the caress, but then it calmed and allowed him to stroke the whole of its face, from the forelock down to its lips.

It had a beautiful face and, when it looked at him, the firelight played in its big eyes. Imagine whipping a horse and blinding it the way Wolfgang had done! What a beast he was. The priest at home always talked about forgiving your enemies. Well, he would never forgive Wolfgang for what he had done to him. He hated him.

He patted the horse's cheek and then pressed his face against its neck, whispering softly, "There, there."

The horse's neck, so warm and soft, made him yearn for home. He could almost feel the comfort of Mama's arm around him. As he ran his hand over the heavy muscles on the horse's shoulder, he thought of Papa—his broad, strong back and his rough working hands that sometimes unexpectedly brushed your cheek with such surprising tenderness. Jozef's trusting eyes, Dorota's loving hugs, Alexy's friendly face, Stefan and Maria jumping on his back for a ride, and the twins planting wet kisses on his cheek. He missed it all.

The fire began to die down and he crouched next to the embers, trying to catch their last warmth, as the night pressed closer and closer. Every sigh of the wind, every rustle in the trees made his senses tingle with fear and he held the ax tightly.

When he heard distant footsteps, he stood up and backed away to the barge so no one could attack him from behind. The footsteps came nearer, then stopped. Leo held his breath. There was a long, long silence. Finally, he couldn't stand it any longer.

"Who's there?" he called.

Silence.

"I've got an ax," he said, trying to sound strong and determined.

"Where's the damned fire?" came the bargeman's slurred voice. "I can't see a blasted thing."

"It's gone out," Leo called, and then ran along the towpath. He found the man sitting, facing the wrong way. He had a bottle in his hand, and his breath stank of vodka as Leo helped him to his feet. Together, they stumbled back toward the barge.

"Ah, there he is—the Preacher," the man said, swinging his bottle toward the horse as they passed. "Doesn't like me drinking, that one. I can see it in his eyes. Probably says his horsey prayers for my soul. But he's a good old horse. Best horse on the canal. Better than one of those smelly, noisy motor barges any day. Ooof!"

He collapsed to the ground and crawled over to the remains of the fire.

"You let it go out, you useless little sparrow," he said, poking the ashes with his bottle. Some sparks leaped up. "No, look—it's still alive. Quick. There's kindling and logs under the tarpaulin at the back of the barge."

Leo ran to fetch the wood and, with much puffing at the embers, he got the flames dancing again. The man took a long swig of vodka to celebrate.

"Well done, Sparrow—you're not as useless as you look. Want a pull of vodka? No? No, that's right—you stay off it. Rots your guts and brain. We're lonely fools who drink it. Lonely fools." He stared gloomily at the fire as if saddened by his own words. "What about you, Sparrow? What are you doing wandering around on your lonesome?"

It was a gentle inquiry, and the old man's face was filled with sympathy, so Leo told him everything—the winter disasters at home, the trouble at the Manor, his hope for a new life in America. The man listened to it all, taking swigs from his bottle, staring at the fire, muttering angrily when Leo talked about Wolfgang and Borys, and nodding when Leo described how he felt leaving his family.

The telling took a long time, and the man was silent at the end of the story. He sat there shaking his head, in what looked a sorrowful fashion, so Leo was astonished when he suddenly screamed, "Stupid!"

He leaned over and grabbed Leo's shirt, dragging him close. "You stupid, stupid boy! Look at my life. Alone with the Preacher. No one to care. She went off, didn't she? Strangled weasel, she said. Yeah, well, I'd strangle her if I got the chance."

His eyes were huge and crazy as he ranted, and spittle flew from his lips. Leo struggled to try to get away, but the man grabbed his throat.

"And what are you? A refugee. Knock-knocking on doors. 'Oh, please let me in!' You know what they'll do? They'll spit in your face and trample on your dream. They don't need you. There are millions of you, wandering the face of the earth, begging to be let in."

"Don't! Don't!" Leo gasped as the man's fingers dug deeper into his throat.

"Leave home, and you leave everything. You're alone among strangers who only care about themselves. You're just scum to them—scum that wants to steal their jobs, steal their houses, and steal their women! You don't understand. You can't trust anyone. They'll only let you down."

Tears suddenly filled the man's eyes, and he relaxed his grip on Leo's throat. He stared away into the night, and his voice softened. "There's no mercy in them, Sparrow. No love. They'll eat you alive—a poor little kid like you. This world is a bitter, cruel place. We'd all be better off out of it."

He let go of Leo, and the tears toppled over the rims of his eyes and trickled down his cheek. He lifted his hand to wipe them away and tumbled backward. He tried to sit up again, but it was too much for him and he slumped back and closed his eyes. A few seconds later, he began snoring.

Slowly, Leo got to his feet and tiptoed away.

A mist was rising from the canal and swirling across the

towpath. The moon was low in the sky, but its light was bright. It caught the coiling mist, making it glow. Soon he was walking knee-deep through a silvery cloud and he couldn't see where the towpath ended and where the canal began, so he climbed the embankment and walked along the top for nearly half an hour before he felt he was far enough away from the man. There were no sheltering trees up here and the grass was wet with dew but he didn't fancy sleeping down in the shadowy woods on the other side of the embankment. He lay down and stared at the mist glowing in the moonlight until his eyes grew heavy, and he drifted away.

It was still dark when he woke—the moon had set, and there was no sign of daybreak in the east. He sat up and shivered. He was soaking wet and his body ached as he got to his feet. The first few paces hurt his knees and ankles but he kept moving and gradually the stiffness eased. The mist had risen to near the top of the embankment, so he was walking, cold and alone, above a flat, featureless landscape that matched the gray, empty feeling that gripped his heart.

Perhaps the man was right. Perhaps the world was a cruel and bitter place—a world full of strangers who only cared about themselves, a world that would trample his dreams.

He trudged on, head down, seeing nothing, and continuing on only because he didn't know what else to do.

A breeze blew his hair and, when he looked up, he saw that the mist was thinning and light was beginning to creep across the horizon. From close by, a blackbird began to sing. Its voice was so sweet and its melody so full of unexpected trills that Leo felt a chuckle rise in his chest.

Now the night was retreating, and the new world started to take shape as the sky lit up, reflecting in the canal. Its waters stretched away into the distance, shimmering under the last wisps of the mist and showing him the way. Other birds were joining the blackbird's song—thrushes and warblers, and then a skylark, soaring somewhere high above. As the chorus swelled, the tip of the rising sun burst above the horizon, illuminating the trees in the meadows and melting the chill that had filled Leo's heart.

He walked more briskly now, and a short while later, he came across another barge tied up to the towpath. Three young children were playing on the grass while their parents busied themselves around the fire, preparing the breakfast. The oldest boy, about six, had a puppy in his arms and when he placed it on the ground it came bounding up the embankment toward Leo.

"Hello, little thing," Leo laughed, bending down and holding out his hand to the puppy, who stopped to yap at him before rushing back to his young master.

The adults looked up from their tasks and waved. Leo waved back and set off again.

He had only gone a short distance when he heard footsteps behind him. He turned and saw the little boy running toward him with his puppy bounding along at his heels.

"Mummy says it's for you," the boy said shyly, holding out a chunk of bread.

Leo took it. "Thank you," he started to say, but the boy was already dashing away down the slope. "Thank you!" he called to the woman, who was standing by the fire. "Thank you!"

"For your journey," she called back. "Godspeed."

He nodded, his throat too tight to speak, and then he set off again.

Chapter 12

Leo arrived on the outskirts of Bromberg in the early afternoon and was immediately lost in a blur of noise, movement, and smells. Carriages and carts clattered past on roads that reeked of horse dung and urine. Factories roared and hissed and banged, their chimneys spewing columns of acrid smoke. Sirens hooted. Barges creaked and boomed as the water cascaded in and out of the locks from the canal into the River Brahe. Whistles shrieked and wheels rattled as trains steamed in and out of the huge station.

The whole town was a whirl of motion, with people everywhere—running, walking, talking, shouting, laughing, and cursing. The busiest market days in Nakel were calm and quiet compared to the jostle and hubbub of the crowds in Bromberg. Even when people were standing, talking to each other, their feet tapped impatiently and their eyes roved everywhere, as if they couldn't wait to end the conversation and join in the bustle again. It was so different from the world Leo was used to, a world where people took their time to look and to listen, and where the sight of a stranger was a remarkable event. Here, he passed through the crowds, looking into eyes that didn't look back at him until he felt as if he were invisible.

All afternoon, he rambled in a daze through the narrow streets of old Bromberg and then out into the squares and the broad avenues of the newer part of town. It was only when the light began to fade and the crowds thinned out that he realized how much time he'd wasted. He hadn't found work, and he had nowhere to sleep. The shops and stalls were closing, and people were hurrying home. Factories and workshops were shut. The frantic activity on the docks had stopped, and the cargoes on the barges had been battened down for the night.

He wandered through the center of town, where the restaurants and taverns were crowded with customers. He stood outside one of the bigger restaurants, gazing through the window at the people eating in the candlelit room. The cutlery and glasses sparkled on the white tablecloths, and the dishes were piled with food. One of the waiters came out and shooed him away from the window, saying that he was annoying the diners, so he walked across the square and onto a bridge over the River Brahe. A man was lighting the gas lamps along the bank and Leo stared at the slide and shiver of the lights on the water.

Suddenly there was a burst of noise and a platoon of soldiers came marching around the corner into the square and onto the bridge. They were led by a drummer, and the rattle of the drum and the pounding of the boots sent a thrill through Leo—a war machine. He had heard that phrase before, and now he knew what it meant. These soldiers—marching three abreast, in perfect unison, and splendid in their smart uniforms—would strike fear into any enemy.

A man strolling across the bridge raised his hat and cried, "Long live King Wilhelm!" Others took up the cry, and as the soldiers drew level, Leo joined in.

"Long live King Wilhelm!" he shouted, and one of the soldiers flashed a smile at him and winked.

It was the first friendly gesture he had seen all day, and as the soldiers marched away, Leo ran along the pavement and fell into step beside them, imitating the swing and swagger of their movements.

They turned left along the river and then wheeled right, across the broad avenue and up a long street toward the station. And still Leo marched alongside them, wishing he could be like them—so proud and purposeful.

When they finally got to the big square in front of the station, there were already hundreds of soldiers milling around. The platoon came to a halt, and their commander dismissed them. They swung their packs and rifles from their shoulders, took off their helmets, and relaxed. Some headed for the stalls selling food and drinks, some lit cigarettes or pipes and fell into conversation, and others sat down on the pavement and leaned against the buildings, stretching their muscles and undoing their boots to cool their aching feet.

Leo wandered among them, catching fragments of their chatter. "…Who wants some snuff?…Berlin? I thought we were going to France…My grandfather told me you should pour vodka on lice… Didn't you see her? Beautiful, she was…Cut his finger off with his bayonet! I reckon he didn't fancy dodging bullets…"

The soldier who had smiled at him was sitting on the far side of the square, eating with a group of friends, and he smiled again as Leo walked past.

"Look, it's our little cadet," he called. "You want some rations after all that marching? Don't be shy. We've got some to spare, haven't we, lads?"

The other men nodded, so Leo sat down on the pavement next to them. The soldier cut a chunk of salami and handed it to him with some bread.

"Thank you, sir," Leo said, taking a big bite of salami.

"Sir? I'm not an officer yet! Konrad's the name. So, you planning to join the army, littl'un?"

Leo laughed and shrugged.

"It's a great life!" one of the soldiers said. "Good food, fancy uniform, and all the women itching to kiss you!"

"Yeah, and a fine funeral when one of the Frenchies sticks his bayonet in your guts," Konrad added, and they all laughed.

"Are you going to war?" Leo mumbled, his mouth full of bread.

"Looks like it," Konrad said. "King Wilhelm thinks the French insulted him because they wouldn't let one of his cousins become king of Spain."

"No, that's not it," one of the other men said. "It's Bismarck. He's a deep one, our prime minister. He's picking a fight with the French so he can get all the German states together in a war. Then he can take control of the whole lot, and make Prussia top dog."

"Well, whatever the reason, Wilhelm's sending us to teach the Frenchies a lesson," Konrad said.

"Will you see him…the King?" Leo asked, and was surprised when the soldiers roared with laughter.

"No, it's a funny thing, that," Konrad explained. "The high-ups love picking a fight, but they're never around when the killing starts. It's always poor fools like us who do the bleeding and dying for them."

Konrad volunteered to get drinks for the others, and Leo went with him. As they stood in the long line, Konrad asked if he lived in Bromberg.

"No, I come from Wilhelmsdorf—it's near Nakel. I'm going to the sea."

"The sea? How are you planning to get there?"

"Walk, I suppose. Do you know where it is?"

"That's a fine start! You're going to the sea but don't even know where it is!" Konrad chuckled. "Well, the nearest sea is the Baltic, so I reckon you'd be best off following the River Wisła down to Danzig. But it's a devil of a long walk. Don't you think you'd be better off at home?"

Leo shook his head.

"I see. Well, I daresay you've got your reasons. Still, I wouldn't like my eldest lad roaming the country like that. He's about your age. The minute I spotted you on the bridge, you reminded me of him. What a spark he is. I just want to get through this damn war in one piece so I can go home and see him and his two little sisters. God willing."

Konrad crossed himself and fell silent for a moment, lost in his thoughts. Then he turned to Leo, and his eyes were glistening.

"There are a lot of ways to die, lad, and none of them are good. Now listen, I've promised myself that my boy won't grow up without a father, so I'm going to take real good care of myself when it comes to the fighting. And I want you to do the same on this journey of yours. Don't ask me why, but I've got a funny feeling that if you stay safe, I'll be safe. So I'm counting on you, do you hear me?"

Leo nodded.

"Good," Konrad said. He stared intently at Leo, and then a smile swept the serious look off his face. "We're going to be all right, you and me. I can feel it in my bones."

When they got back with the drinks, one of the soldiers gave Leo some beer. It tasted horrible but he took a big swig. All the soldiers laughed, so he took another one, and they laughed again and said he was made of the right stuff. Then one of them handed him a bottle of vodka.

"Don't give him that, you'll make a sot of him," Konrad objected. But the others cheered and told him to knock it back, so Leo raised the bottle and drank.

The liquid poured down his throat, and it was only after he'd taken three big gulps that the burning hit him. His throat seemed to be on fire, and tears ran from his eyes as he bent over, coughing and choking.

"Now look what you've done!" Konrad said angrily, snatching the bottle out of Leo's hand.

"It's only a joke," one of the soldiers said. "It'll help to warm him up."

And it was true—as the burning in his throat faded and he stopped coughing, Leo began to feel a warm glow in his belly—a glow that spread upward to his head, making him want to smile.

"There you are—he likes it," the soldier said pointing to him.

And the smile on Leo's face grew wider as they all looked at him. Then he started to laugh and the others joined in. He laughed until his stomach muscles ached, but suddenly, he didn't want to laugh any more. He felt sick. He tried to focus his eyes but the world had started to spin and, when he staggered to his feet, he found that his legs were wobbly and couldn't take his weight. He almost fell over but Konrad caught him and held him.

"Come on, lad, you need a rest," Konrad said, lifting him and carrying him over to a doorway.

Konrad laid him down and Leo closed his eyes. His head was spinning and he thought he was going to be sick, but then he was whirled down into sleep.

At one moment during the night, he was aware of noises—shouts and the stamping of boots—but he turned over and drifted away again. When he woke up, his head was throbbing with pain but he forced his eyes open. In the dim light of the early morning, he could see that the square was empty. The soldiers had gone. He sat up slowly and a piece of paper slipped off his chest. He picked it up and unfolded it. Even before he read it, he knew who it was from and he knew what it would say.

He carefully spelled the words out, the way the priest had taught him. And he was right. Konrad had left him the message—"Stay safe."

Chapter 13

THE POISON HEADACHE FROM THE VODKA LASTED ALL MORNING, and the loud noises of the city pounded in his skull. But he forced himself to keep looking for work. He had to have money—money for food on the journey, money to pay for the ship to America, and perhaps, if he earned enough, money he could send home. He dragged himself from one hot, stuffy building after another—an iron foundry, a machine shop, a flour mill—but the answer was the same each time: no work.

By the middle of the day, he was exhausted from the heat and the throbbing in his head. He sat down under the shade of a tree near the river. There was a cooling breeze along the water. Barges and small boats chugged by, but there was none of the banging and crashing that had stabbed his head all morning. He closed his eyes and dozed off. When he woke up, his mouth was dry and his ear felt numb from leaning against the tree trunk, but the headache was gone.

He found some steps down to the river and splashed water onto his face. Could he drink it? It was dirty and oily, and bits of rubbish bobbed up and down next to the bank but his thirst was so bad that he cupped his hands and slurped mouthful after mouthful. Refreshed, he suddenly felt hopeful. This afternoon, he would smile and look eager and fit. This afternoon, people would look at him and know that he was a good worker. This afternoon, he would get a job. It would be all right.

Even when he got turned down at the first place, a paper mill, he didn't lose heart. And at the wood yard next to the mill, he was given hope. The foreman looked him over and said that he'd be needing extra help when the next delivery of wood came. When Leo asked when that would be, he responded, "In two or three days. There's a raft of over a thousand trunks waiting on the Wisła, but the damned carter is busy. If you come back once the timber starts arriving, you'll have a job for sure."

Leo couldn't stop smiling as he walked back toward the center of town. He had a job. True, it didn't start for two or three days, but he had a job. In the meantime, though, how would he eat, and where would he sleep?

He wandered the streets aimlessly, looking at the food in the shops. As he was gazing into the window of a baker's shop, he saw the reflection of a woman in the glass and his heart jumped. It was Mama, coming toward him. But when he spun around, he saw his mistake: the woman was the same size as Mama and had the same color hair—even walked rather like her—but she was a stranger. Her face was harder than Mama's, and her eyes looked straight past him at something in the shop window instead of lighting up with love the way Mama's would.

The woman went in to buy some bread, and when she came out, he followed her. It was silly, really, but it made him feel a bit less lonely. He watched her as she moved from stall to stall in the busy marketplace, looking carefully at the vegetables and ending up buying onions, a cabbage, some carrots, and a bunch of parsley.

Then she made her way through the crowds into the covered market and bought a small rabbit. The butcher gave her some paper, and she put it into her basket and laid the rabbit on top. A small bead of blood oozed from its mouth, and its large, dead eyes stared at Leo as he followed the woman out of the echoey building. Night was already falling over the town, and he stopped and watched her quickly disappear from view up the dark, cobbled lane. He imagined the family waiting for her, and he felt a sudden longing for his own home. He turned and ran in the opposite direction, trying to shake off the sadness of it.

He ran through the square, across the river bridge, and then up the avenue toward the station. Perhaps there would be another friendly soldier who would give him food, another group of men to talk to and laugh with. But the square in front of the station was empty. He lay down in the same doorway and, despite the hunger in his belly, fell asleep.

"Get up!" a voice was saying as he jerked awake. He felt a kick on the back of his leg. "Get up, I said!"

Leo scrambled to his feet, and the policeman grabbed him. "I'm not having vagrants like you hanging around on my beat. Get lost and don't come back. Understand?"

Leo nodded, and the policeman pushed him so roughly that he stumbled down the three steps and almost fell onto the pavement. He stood there for a second, still half asleep, but when the policeman started down the steps after him, he ran along the pavement and dodged into the first alleyway.

He waited for a while and then peered around the corner. The policeman was strolling away down the main avenue, so he ran across the square toward the lights of the station. He pushed open the big main door and went into the booking hall. Two railway officials were standing by the ticket office; they looked at him suspiciously, so he turned around and went outside again.

There was a small café, little more than a wooden hut, next to the main station building. It was closed, but he ducked around the back to see if any food had been thrown out. It was dark behind the hut, and Leo was startled by a noise from the shadows. A tramp had had the same idea and was scrabbling in the rubbish bin. There was a grunt of satisfaction. The tramp stuffed something in his mouth and then bent down to search the bin again. He found a few more scraps, which he ate hungrily. Then, he limped toward Leo.

"Sorry, lad. It's all gone," he muttered as he went past. The man had long, matted hair, and there was a terrible smell coming from his filthy clothes. But his "Sorry, lad" was friendly, so Leo decided to follow him.

The tramp got to the end of the road and turned onto a narrow path that ran along a fence by the side of the railway lines. The path was narrow, and the bright moonlight showed a steep drop on one side. Leo walked carefully, running his hand along the fence for safety. The tramp suddenly veered left and disappeared into the shadows. When Leo got to that spot he saw a narrow track winding down the slope through the trees. He took it, treading warily in the darkness. He could hear the tramp's footsteps ahead, but after about fifty meters, he realized they had stopped. He stood still listening, and then there was a rustle behind him. An arm snaked around his neck and pulled him back into the bushes.

"Who are you? What do you want?" the tramp's voice hissed.

"Just looking for somewhere to sleep," Leo said, almost gagging on the stench from the man's clothes.

The tramp grunted and let him go.

"I'll ask the others," he said. "Wait here."

He plunged into the bushes, and Leo heard a muffled conversation.

"You don't tell no one else about this place, right?" the tramp whispered when he came back.

"All right," Leo said, and then followed him up through the bushes to where the slope overhung them, forming a kind of cave. He ducked down and went inside. Three dark shapes were huddled on the ground, already settling back into sleep.

Leo got on his hands and knees and crawled over to the far corner. The tramp lay down nearby and fell asleep almost at once, his snores joining in the chorus from the other sleepers. Despite the noise and the overpowering smell that hung in the small space, Leo was happy to stay. He had company. He wasn't alone.

A short time later, a storm broke over the south side of Bromberg. Leo watched the lightning and counted the seconds between the flashes and the rolls of thunder. The storm was coming nearer. Rain started to fall heavily—he could hear it slapping down on the leaves outside, but he was dry under the overhang and he drifted off to sleep, feeling safe and lucky.

He woke before the others and crawled out of the den into the new morning. Drops of water still dripped from the trees, and his waistcoat was wet by the time he got back to the top path.

He made his way down into the center of town, heading for the marketplace. He would offer to help one of the traders to carry crates, sweep up, or anything else, as long as they gave him some food.

He was walking past one of the crossroads in the narrow lanes of the old town when a boy came charging around the corner and bumped into him.

"I went that way," the boy said, pointing to an alleyway on the left. Then he darted off in the other direction and ducked into a doorway.

Leo was still trying to work out what he meant when he heard the sound of pounding feet and two men came running around the corner.

"Did you see a boy?" one of them asked, grabbing hold of him.

"Yes," Leo said and pointed down the alleyway on the left, "He went that way."

The men sped off, and a moment later the boy came out from his hiding place and beckoned. He held out his hand as Leo approached and his face cracked into a big smile, showing two gaps in his front teeth.

"You saved my bacon! Thanks!" He grabbed Leo's hand and shook it enthusiastically. "We're going to be best friends. I know it! Come on. Let's get away before those two lumps come back."

And that's how Tomasz came into Leo's life.

Chapter 14

LEO TROTTED ALONGSIDE TOMASZ THROUGH A MAZE OF NARROW lanes until they reached the top of the hill where there was a little park that looked down over the roofs of the town to the River Brahe. Two large chestnut trees stood in the middle of the little park, and between them was a large bronze statue of a man. Tomasz sat down on the base of the statue and Leo sat next to him.

"This is my favorite place in the whole of Bromberg," Tomasz said. "Nice and quiet—hardly anyone ever comes here. And I've got this old fellow for company. Can you read?"

"A bit."

"What does it say?" he asked, pointing to the writing on the plinth.

"Stanislaw Trembecki, 1740–1812," Leo spelled out.

"Oh, him."

"Who was he?"

"Never heard of him!" Tomasz grinned. "He's a nice old chap, but he doesn't look very jolly, does he? When they make statues of me, I'm going to look much happier than him."

"Statues of you!" Leo chuckled.

"Yes. I'm going to be famous one day. Besides, I'm the son of a count, and counts always have statues made of them."

Tomasz said it so seriously that Leo didn't know whether to laugh or not, so he changed the conversation. "Why were those men chasing you?"

"Oh, they thought I stole something from their stall."

"Did you?" Leo asked.

"A meat pie and two apples. I ask you—would you bother to chase someone for nearly twenty minutes because of a little meat pie and two apples? Anyway, we've got something to eat now." And with a flourish, he pulled the food from inside his jacket. He broke the meat pie and handed half to Leo, along with one of the apples.

"Mmm, not bad," Tomasz mumbled as he wolfed his part of the pie.

"It's delicious," Leo said, trying to eat slowly so he could savor every bite.

"Good apples too. I think I'll always get my food from that stall," Tomasz laughed.

When he finished eating, Leo lay back and looked up at the blue sky. For the first time in days, he felt relaxed. His belly wasn't growling, the sun was warm, and the smell of flowers was wafting on the breeze. Tomasz began humming a familiar tune, and when he finished that one, he hummed another, and then another. Leo closed his eyes and listened to the songs. Sometimes Tomasz sang words to the tunes, often starting off with lines that Leo recognized, such as the old song:

"Plenty of prayers, plenty of food
Never does harm, always does good."

But then Tomasz added words that he'd obviously made up:

"I've got a friend, we met in the street
But friendship is sweet wherever you meet
He saved me from men who wanted my blood
We went to a park and I gave him some food."

"You've got a good voice," Leo said when Tomasz finally stopped singing.

"I have, haven't I?" Tomasz replied. "I might be a musician one day, a famous singer, or a great pianist. Or a violinist—I like the violin. Or I could be a poet, because I'm good at making up lines."

"Where did you learn to do that?"

"From my father. He's a cobbler, and while he's repairing shoes he sings the old songs and makes up words about the people the shoes belong to. He's brilliant at it—sometimes he makes up funny lines, and other times he sings really sad lines that can make you almost cry."

"I thought you said your father was a count," Leo said, laughing and pointing an accusing finger at Tomasz.

"He is," Tomasz said.

"How can he be a cobbler and a count?"

"Aha," Tomasz said, tapping the side of his nose with his finger.

"I caught you out! I caught you out!" Leo teased.

But Tomasz ignored him. He jumped to his feet and walked away. Leo thought he'd offended him, but after a few paces Tomasz glanced back and called, "Well, come on, then."

In fact, Leo came to learn that it was impossible to offend Tomasz. Insults or unkind words just bounced off him. It was the same with bad events or setbacks—he seemed to let them roll over him and then he carried on as if nothing had happened. So when they got back into town, Tomasz decided they should try begging for a while to get some money. He knelt down on a street corner and made Leo do the same.

Leo burned with embarrassment, kneeling there with his hands cupped in front of him, and he couldn't bear to meet the eyes of the people walking past. But Tomasz threw himself into it, stretching his arms out and giving beseeching looks to the passersby. And at the end of half an hour, when they hadn't been given a single coin, he simply got to his feet, brushed the dirt off his knees, and announced that it wasn't a good day for begging but that it would be better tomorrow.

As they were walking past the timber yard, Leo told him about the job he had been promised, and Tomasz immediately decided to go in and see if he could get work too. The foreman was sitting on a stool just inside the gate, and he yawned and waved his hand dismissively as soon as Tomasz started to ask about a job. Tomasz smiled and went on talking as if he hadn't noticed, and when he mentioned that he had spent two years at Barbitzki's timber yard in Posen, the foreman suddenly looked up.

"Barbitzki's?" he asked. "That's a big mill."

Tomasz nodded. "One of the biggest. Old Ambrozy said I was the best young worker he'd ever had. You know Ambrozy—the foreman there? No? Well, he's heard of you, all right—he told me that you were the only boss worth working for in Bromberg. I know I'm small, but I'm much stronger than I look. Give me a try and you won't be disappointed. I can haul and carry and chop and saw with the best of 'em."

"Well, you're keen—I'll grant you that," the foreman said with a laugh. "All right, I've already promised your raggedy friend there, so I suppose I could give you a chance too. The delivery's due the day after tomorrow. Come back then, and I might have a couple of weeks' work for you."

Leo waited until they were outside the gates before he asked, "Hey, is all that stuff about Barbitzki's true?"

"Of course." Tomasz smiled. "It's one of the biggest mills in Posen."

"And you worked there?"

"Well, not exactly—but they used to haul timber from the woods near my village and I used to go and pick up the chippings for our stove!"

"You little liar!" Leo laughed. "And Ambrozy?"

"First name I could think of!"

"Your tongue will come up in blisters. One for every lie."

"Nah, that's just an old tale," Tomasz said. "Anyway, they weren't lies—just a bit of grease to help the wheel go around smoothly. Where's the harm? 'People are like dogs, Tom—stroke 'em, and they'll eat out of your hand.' That's what my father always says."

"Which father is that—the cobbler or the count?" Leo joked.

Tomasz ignored the jibe and went on. "Make people feel good, and they'll be good to you. It's all right for you, of course—you don't even have to try. Those big eyes and that big smile—you could charm the birds down from the trees."

"What are you talking about?" Leo laughed.

"Look at me. How old do you think I am?"

"Eleven?"

"See! I'm fourteen! Fourteen! I've got a beard—look," Tomasz said, pointing to a couple of wispy hairs on his chin. "And I've got some around my you-know-what too. I'm practically a man, but I don't look any bigger than you. I'll grow, of course—I'm going to be really tall in a couple of years, but let's face it, at the moment, I'm a bit of short-ass. Look at my ears—huge and sticking out! And my hair—with this stupid sticking-up bit," he said, pressing the offending tuft of hair down and then removing his hand to show how it popped up again. "Luckily, I'm smart, so I know how to make people like me. That's why we'll be a good team—you with the looks, and me with the brains. Hey, wait a minute…"

He stopped and took a couple of steps back. He peered down the side path of a big house and then glanced up and down the street.

"What?" Leo asked.

Tomasz put his finger to his lips and pulled Leo along the path toward the back garden of the house. Washing was hanging on the line, and Tomasz headed straight for it.

"Don't just stand there. Get the stuff down the other end," he whispered as he started to pull some clothes from the line.

Leo ran to the end of the line and reached up to unpeg a sheet. The wind blew, and the big sheet flapped up over his head. He panicked, pulling it wildly to get it off his face.

"Not that! Just the shirts and dresses," Tomasz hissed.

But Leo was so nervous that his hands were shaking. He managed to unpeg only two shirts before Tomasz whistled and jerked his head in the direction of the road. They were tiptoeing toward the side path when the back door suddenly banged open and a woman came running out of the house, shrieking, "Hey! What are you doing?"

Tomasz managed to dodge past her down the path, but Leo was trapped. He looked around quickly—the garden wall was too high to climb. He threw the two shirts at the woman and, as she reached to catch them, he darted toward the open back door.

He found himself in a dark scullery. He ran through it and up a flight of stone stairs into a long corridor. At the far end, light was coming through the stained glass panels of the front door and shining on the polished wooden floor. He charged along the corridor, skidding on a rug halfway along. He crashed down and found himself looking into the doorway of a room.

A little boy, not much more than a baby, was sitting on the floor, dressed in a sailor suit. The boy looked up in surprise and then laughed at Leo sprawled on the rug. There was a line of dribble from the boy's red lips, and Leo instantly knew he was teething. The boy held out his arms, asking to be carried, and for a brief moment Leo was transported home to all those times when his young sisters and brothers had made the same trusting gesture and he had gladly picked them up.

There was a noise behind him, and the woman appeared at the top of the stairs. He scrambled to his feet, ran to the front door, pulled it open, and dashed down the steps to the pavement. Tomasz was waiting for him about fifty meters down the street, the stolen washing bundled up in his arms.

"Didn't you bring those shirts?" Tomasz asked as they ran away. "You're useless!"

They ran all the way to the market and found a clothes stall with an old woman sitting next to it, smoking a pipe. She took it out of her mouth as they approached. "Hello, cherubs. What you got there, then?"

She put the pipe on the side of the stall, picked up a set of wooden teeth, and popped them into her mouth. She clicked the teeth together as she sorted through the bundle. Then, she took them out again and laid them back on the stall, as if she had only needed them to examine the clothes. She fumbled in her apron pocket and pulled out two coins.

"Two pfennigs? Is that all?" Tomasz asked. "This is good stuff."

"I know, cherub, but they're hard to sell, seeing as where they comes from," the old woman said, winking and putting her pipe back in her mouth. She took a big puff and breathed the foul-smelling smoke toward them. "Take it or leave it."

Tomasz sighed as he held out his hand, and the woman dropped the coins into it.

"She's an old thief," he whispered as they walked away. Then he cheered up. "Still, it'll buy us some bread, so we won't starve to death today! And we'll go and see Emilia. She's works at the Café Bristol on Mostowa Street. I met her a week ago when I first got here. She lets me sleep in the hut at the back of the café, but she's been away the last couple of nights, so I couldn't go. She's adorable. I think she's a bit in love with me!"

They hung around the café until they saw the last customer leave. Tomasz knocked on the kitchen door, and Emilia opened it.

"Two of you? This isn't a home for waifs and strays, Tom," she said, but there was a smile on her lips and a twinkle in her eye.

"Go on, Emmy. It's Leo, he's a good lad. You'll like him."

Emilia sighed and opened the door wider. "Well all right. But no more, Tom. Two's the limit."

"Cross my heart and hope to die," Tomasz said. "You're a gem, my little Em!"

Emilia laughed at the rhyme as she led them through the empty kitchen and into the backyard. She opened the door to a hut and showed them inside.

"Back in a moment," she said.

"See," Tomasz said, with a grand gesture around the hut, "we can move a couple of these old tables, and put some of these cushions on the floor so we can stretch out. Perfect."

A few minutes later, the door opened and Emilia entered with some food that had been left over at the end of the evening. There were two thin slices of ham, a small chunk of cheese, and a couple of cold potatoes.

"I'll have to bolt the door from the outside, or the boss'll notice. Don't look so worried, Leo," she chuckled, brushing her lips quickly across his cheeks. "I'll be back to let you out tomorrow morning. You'll be as snug as a bug in a rug."

"Here, don't kiss him," Tomasz said. "I'm your boyfriend, not him!"

"Oooh, feeling jealous, Tommo? There—a big smacker for you too! 'Night 'night, boys. See you in the morning."

Emilia closed the door, and they heard her slide the bolt into place. They ate the scraps of food, spread some cushions on the floor, and lay down.

Leo closed his eyes. The softness of the cushions, the warmth of the hut, and the nearness of a friend—it was luxury, and he was almost instantly asleep.

He woke briefly during the night and lay listening to Tomasz, who seemed to be having a bad dream—he was whimpering, and at one moment, he mumbled, "No, leave me alone." Then he was quiet again, and Leo turned over and went back to sleep.

Chapter 15

WHEN EMILIA OPENED THE HUT THE NEXT MORNING, SHE brought some bread and cake and a mug of coffee for each of them. After days of worrying where the next food was coming from, it was great to start the day with a big breakfast, and Emilia promised that she'd save some leftovers for them when the café closed at the end of the evening. It didn't stop Tomasz from suddenly deciding to grab a dried sausage as they were passing a stall in the market, though, which led to another chase up and down the alleyways until they lost their pursuers.

"What did you do that for?" Leo panted when they finally collapsed on the riverbank on the outskirts of town.

"I need plenty of food if I'm going to grow, don't I?" Tomasz laughed, taking out his knife and cutting a big chunk of sausage for himself.

"You'll get caught one day. Everyone will be on the lookout for us now."

"Oh, don't worry about that. Have some—it's delicious," Tomasz said, handing over the sausage and his knife.

"Hellfire! This is sharp," Leo said as the knife sliced through the sausage.

Tomasz grunted and looked away across the river.

"G.N.?" Leo said, noticing the initials carved on the bone handle of the knife. "Who's that?"

"The man I got it from," Tomasz said.

"Oh, I see. You didn't steal it, by any chance?" Leo chuckled as he handed the knife back. Tomasz flashed a fierce glance at him, and the atmosphere suddenly became tense.

Leo didn't know what to say, and they ate in silence. Even when they'd finished, the stiff silence went on, and Tomasz continued to stare across the water until something attracted his attention near his feet. He picked up the knife and looked at it for a moment before beginning to slice small strips off the sausage and dropping them onto the ground.

"What are you doing?" Leo asked, glad to have a chance to speak.

"Feeding the ants," Tomasz said, beaming a big smile at Leo. He was his usual self again. "Come and look."

A column of ants was streaming out of a small hole in the ground and spreading out in all directions along the riverbank. As the shavings of sausage fell among them, the ants scurried around tugging at them, lifting pieces much bigger than themselves and carrying them away toward the hole.

"They're amazing," Tomasz said. "Look at the little things. Imagine how strong they must be to carry bits like that. And you see what they're doing? They're not gobbling it all themselves—they're taking it back to the nest, so they can all share it. And look at those two, helping each other. That's what people should be like."

Tomasz dropped the last bit of sausage and smiled as the ants began to struggle with it. They stayed there, watching the swarming ants until all the food had been dragged down into the hole. Then they got up and walked slowly along the riverbank toward the town.

"A cemetery!" Tomasz said as they passed a gate set in the middle of a long, tall wall. "Let's go and have a look."

It was a bright, sunny day, but Leo felt colder in the cemetery than he had outside the walls. It made his flesh creep to think of all the dead bodies lying just underneath the ground—bones and skulls. Perhaps evil spirits lingered here, even in daytime.

"Oh, come on, Tom, let's go," he said. "It's boring."

"No, it's not. I love cemeteries. You can read the names and dates and imagine the people's lives. Look at this one. Suzanne Gaebel. Oh, look—six of her children died before she did. And her husband too. Poor thing. I hope she was the jolly type and went on enjoying herself. I mean, there's no point in being sad, is there? Life's too short."

"I'm going," Leo said. "I'll wait for you outside."

He sat on the grass bank opposite the cemetery and settled down for a long wait, but a couple of minutes later Tomasz came bursting out of the gate with a terrified expression on his face. He tore away along the track and Leo ran after him.

"What is it?" Leo asked when they finally stopped.

"There was a tomb," Tomasz said. "It was open, and it didn't have a name on it."

"So?"

"It was like it was waiting for someone."

"Who?"

Tomasz looked back toward the cemetery. "I thought it was me," he whispered hoarsely.

Leo shivered.

They hurried along the path, and Tomasz kept glancing nervously over his shoulder. Then, suddenly, he stopped in his tracks and spat on the ground.

"Idiot! It can't be me!" He turned to Leo. "Have you ever been to a fortune teller? Oh, you should! I went to see this old gypsy when I was in Posen. She made me drip this special oil into a bowl of hot water, and it all split up into bits and she read the patterns."

"How?"

"I don't know. But it was incredible. She told me things about my village, things that she couldn't possibly have known. Then she said the oil was glowing and golden, and that meant I was going to be rich one day. But the thing that really made my hair stand on end—she made me shake the bowl, and then she peered at the oil again and told me I was going on a long journey on water. Honestly, I got goose bumps all over."

"Why?"

"Because the day before I saw her, I'd made up my mind that I was going to America. Isn't that amazing?"

"America?" Leo gasped, grabbing Tomasz's arm. "That's where I'm going!"

Tomasz's face lit up in a huge smile. "You see? That proves the gypsy was telling the truth. Nothing bad can happen to me here, because I'm going on a long journey across water—to America. With you! We'll go together. Oh, Leo! We'll help each other, and we'll become rich and famous. And we'll have such happy lives. Can't you just see it?"

Tomasz pulled him into a bear hug and there, in the sunlight, on the bank of the river, they jumped up and down in excitement at the thought of the wonderful future that lay ahead of them.

Chapter 16

THAT EVENING EMILIA BROUGHT THEM SOME COLD MEAT AND potatoes that had been left over in the kitchen. Then she said good night and locked them in the hut for the night.

"I've been thinking about the timber yard tomorrow," Tomasz said while they ate the food. "The man said there'd be a couple of weeks' work, didn't he? Well, if we save all our wages, I reckon we'll have enough to buy tickets for the train to Danzig. And once we're there, it'll be easy to find a ship going to America."

"But how much will the ship cost?"

"We won't pay! We'll work. They're always looking for sailors."

"How do you know?" Leo asked.

"It's obvious. There are ships every day, and there can't be enough sailors for all of them, can there? So they let you do jobs on board, and you don't have to pay your fare. I know lots of people who've done it."

"Who?" Leo asked.

"Oh, people. Anyway, I'm tired. I want to sleep. Good night."

It was obvious that the idea of getting a free voyage was just Tomasz hoping and dreaming, but as Leo drifted off to sleep, he couldn't help hoping and dreaming too. Danzig. A ship to America. A life of riches, and money to send home to Mama and Papa.

Perhaps if he believed hard enough, it would come true.

Leo awoke to the sound of knocking. He turned over and saw Tomasz banging on the door.

"What are you doing?" he asked, sitting up.

"It's day," Tomasz said, pointing to the strip of light under the door. "We've got to go to work."

He began banging on the door again and calling Emilia's name, but no one came.

"Don't worry," Leo said. "She'll be here soon."

"We're going to be late," Tomasz said, and went on banging. Still no one came and finally he stopped and sat down on the floor, jiggling his feet impatiently. About half an hour later, there was a noise from the yard and he jumped to his feet and started rapping on the door again.

"Come on, Emilia," he cried. "Open up!"

The bolt slid back and light flooded in as the door opened.

"Who the hell are you?" said a man's voice.

They shaded their eyes against the blinding light and saw a large man standing in the doorway.

"It was an accident. We got locked in!" Tomasz said quickly. "We were just looking for somewhere to sleep."

"Oh, yes? You were calling for Emilia. What's she got to do with it?" the man asked.

"I just heard someone say that name after we were locked in, so I thought it must be her," Tomasz said, and Leo was astounded at how quickly he made up the lies.

"So who gave you those?" the man asked, pointing to the empty plates on the floor.

"They were here when we came in, weren't they?"

As if looking for confirmation, Tomasz turned to Leo, mouthed the word "run," and then burst past the man, knocking him to one side. The man was caught by surprise and fell backward. He tried to steady himself but collapsed into the corner, so Leo scooted past him and followed Tomasz out of the door.

They ran across the yard, through the café, and out onto Mostowa Street. They turned left and dashed along the road before ducking into a tangle of alleyways that Tomasz seemed to know by heart. In the distance, a clock was striking seven and Leo realized just how late they were.

As they turned the corner next to the paper mill, they saw the carts lined up along the road and some workers were already unloading the tree trunks and hauling them into the timber yard. The foreman was standing next to the gates supervising the delivery.

"Stack it at the far end, lads—against the wall," he called to two men who were carrying a long pine trunk into the yard.

"I know we're late," Tomasz panted, as they skidded to a halt next to the foreman, "but it won't happen again. We promise! In fact, we're going to sleep here, next to the logs. That way, we'll never be late and we can guard the timber overnight. It'll save you the trouble of hiring guards."

"Far wall, lads," the foreman said to the men carrying the next log.

"We're good workers. Ask the foreman at Barbitzki's," Tomasz said, his voice becoming more desperate as the foreman continued to ignore him. "We'll work late. We'll do anything."

"I've got no place for sluggards," the foreman said, finally bothering to look at them. "We started work at sunrise."

"We were locked in—I swear. Just give us a chance," Tomasz pleaded.

"Too late. I've got a full gang now, and I don't need any more."

"Please," Tomasz begged, snatching at the foreman's sleeve.

"I said…too…late!" the foreman snapped, and then he marched away and disappeared into his office.

"Oh, well," Tomasz said, laying a consoling arm around Leo's shoulder as they slowly made their way back into town. "There are plenty of other jobs. I wager we'll find another one today. Hey, perhaps we could offer to shine soldiers' boots. There are always lots of them waiting for trains, and they'd probably pay well."

They asked at factories and shops, and down on the docks. Nothing. And, unusually, there were no soldiers up near the station. By the end of the morning, even Tomasz was losing hope.

"Let's try the market," Leo suggested.

There was an auction in the grain market, and they went around offering to carry sacks out to the wagons. But no one wanted their help, so they moved on into the packed vegetable market. They were dodging in and out of the crowd when a cart trundled across Leo's path, and he had to stop for a moment while it passed.

When he looked again, Tomasz was already lost in the crush of people, so Leo put his head down and started pushing his way through the throng.

"Sorry," he said, as he bumped into a man coming the other way.

He glanced up and froze.

It was Borys.

A look of surprise flashed across the overseer's face, and then he reached out to grab him. Leo turned and fled, ducking low and pushing people aside in his desperation to get away. He heard a curse and glanced over his shoulder to see Borys struggling to get past a woman carrying a crate of geese.

There was a gap in the crowd to Leo's right, so he dove through it and out into a narrow lane. There were fewer people here, and he tore past the stalls and then took a quick look back.

No sign of Borys.

He skidded into another alley and dashed away.

Chapter 17

LEO KEPT RUNNING, THROUGH THE ALLEYWAYS AND THEN ALONG the long, wide road that led out of Bromberg. When he saw an orchard, he jumped across a ditch and threw himself down in the long grass at the base of an apple tree.

He was gasping for breath, and the blue sky above him jerked and rocked from the pounding of his heart. At last, the burning in his lungs faded, and he raised his head above the long stems of grass to look back toward town.

The road was empty.

He lay down again and thought about Borys. What was the overseer doing in Bromberg? Searching for him? Or just paying one of his usual visits to buy things for the Baron's estate?

Whatever the case, Borys now knew where he was, and he could tell the mayor of Exin. Perhaps the mayor would telegraph the police in Bromberg. Perhaps they would guess he was heading to the sea, and the police would be on the lookout for him everywhere. He felt trapped and helpless.

His only hope was to get away—far away, where his past wouldn't follow him.

But he couldn't go without Tom. Their friendship had changed everything. The dream of going to America had seemed impossible when he was alone, but together, they could make it happen. He had to go back into town and find him, even if meant risking meeting Borys again. It was too dangerous in daylight, so he would have to wait until night.

But suppose he couldn't find Tomasz. Suppose Tomasz gave up looking for him and decided to leave Bromberg on his own. No, he wouldn't do that. Would he?

He tried to keep calm by thinking what he would do if he were searching for Tomasz. He would check the places where they'd been together—the Café Bristol, or the park. Yes, and that's exactly what Tom would do too.

He couldn't wait to see his friend's cheerful face again, but he forced himself to wait through the long, lonely hours until sunset. Then, as night fell, he started back into town.

He avoided bright lights and, keeping his head down, flitted along in the shadows until he reached Mostowa Street. He dodged from dark doorway to dark doorway until he was opposite the Café Bristol. Emilia was serving, and when she came out to clear one of the tables, he ran across to speak to her.

"Get away from here," she said, anxiously looking back into the café. "My boss nearly gave me the sack this morning because of you two."

"It wasn't our fault," Leo said. "He just found us there. And now I've lost Tom."

"Oh, he'll turn up, like a bad penny. He always does," she said.

Her voice had been sharp, but now she looked at him and her face softened. "No. you'll find him, don't worry. But you mustn't come back here—I've got my mother and two young sisters to provide for, so I can't afford to lose this job. But when you find Tom, you two stick together and look after each other, do you hear?"

She ruffled Leo's hair and then hurried back into the café.

The park was his last hope, and he made his way uphill, scared to arrive in case Tomasz wasn't there. He came out into the open space, and his heart sank. The moon had risen, and its cold gray light showed the park was empty. In a panic, he ran over to the statue, hoping Tomasz was sleeping behind it. But he wasn't.

He wandered over to the park's edge and looked down the hill. The cold moon shone up at him from the waters of the River Brahe. The town of Bromberg lay below him—so many streets, so many little alleyways, so many people. He could search for days and never find Tom. And every extra day he stayed, the greater the danger of being found by Borys.

His legs trembled, and he slumped down at the base of the statue, feeling weak. All he'd eaten in the last two days was half a loaf of bread. If Tomasz were here, he'd find some way to get food. He would be lively and optimistic about the future. He'd make up one of his songs, or tell some jokes. But he wasn't here. Perhaps he had already left Bromberg and was making his way to Danzig. A huge sadness gripped Leo's heart at the thought of never seeing his friend again.

He closed his eyes and felt the world slip away.

He was dreaming of Tomasz. He could hear his voice calling him, "Leo, Leo." In his sleep, he felt a deep sob rise up in his chest. Then hands gripped him and shook him awake. He opened his eyes, and there was Tomasz, bending over him, smiling, and calling his name.

"Leo! Where the devil did you go? I thought I'd never find you, you daft dog!"

Tomasz had some food in his pocket, of course, and Leo wolfed down a carrot and a salt biscuit before he started to tell the whole story—Borys, the lambs, the beating, everything.

"Punching a nobleman's son—that's not such a big crime. It's not as if you murdered someone," Tomasz said. There was a pause, and he added, "Not like me."

He seemed absolutely serious and, for a second, Leo believed him. Then he remembered all the other lies and stories.

"Oh, yes, who did you kill?" he joked. "The cobbler? The count? Or was it that foreman at Barbitzki's timber yard, where you never worked?"

Tomasz's face, blue-gray in the moonlight, kept its serious expression for a moment longer. Then it cracked into a grin, and he burst out laughing.

Leo punched him playfully on the arm and joined in the laughter. Good old Tom—always finding ways to cheer him up.

"Right, this is the plan," Tomasz said. "We're going to slip out of town and leave this Borys bloke to stew in his own juices. It's time we went, anyway. We'll never get to Danzig by staying here, will we?"

"But we haven't made any money yet."

"Oh, we'll worry about that tomorrow," Tomasz said. "Something'll turn up."

The next morning, Tomasz decided that Leo should stay in the park, to avoid being seen, while he went into town to find a barge or a wagon heading north to Danzig.

The time dragged on, and Leo found himself going over and over that day when all this had started. If only he hadn't taken those lambs. If only he hadn't hit Wolfgang. He should have done what he was told—gotten on his knees and begged for forgiveness.

No! He could never regret those punches. He'd taken his punishment. Wolfgang had just wanted to humiliate him, to crush him. Well, nobody would ever crush him. Nobody. Wolfgang had gotten what he deserved.

A couple of hours later, Tomasz came running into the park and sat down next to Leo at the base of the statue.

"No luck with the barges or wagons," he panted. "But I think I saw Borys. What does he look like?"

"Big. Wide shoulders, broad face, curly hair the color of oxblood," Leo said.

"That's him! Ugly pig, isn't he? I was going through the marketplace, and I saw him turn and give me a real stare. I just knew it was him. Good thing you didn't come with me."

"I've got to get out of here, Tom. If he's still looking for me…"

"Don't worry. I've come up with a plan. We'll lie low until evening, and then we'll catch a train."

"We haven't got any money!" Leo said.

"Look," Tomasz explained, "you pay your money, you get your ticket, the man checks your ticket, you get on your train, and away you go. Right?"

"I don't know. I've never been on a train."

"Well, trust me. That's what happens. So all we have to do is avoid the man who checks the tickets. It's obvious. I don't know why I didn't think of it before!"

Chapter 18

I N THE EARLY EVENING, THEY LEFT THE PARK, WENT INTO TOWN, crossed the bridge, and hurried along the broad avenue that led up to the station. Leo kept looking left and right, scared they would bump into Borys. But they reached the station without trouble and pushed through the doors into the main hall. It was packed with travelers. They watched as people lined up for their tickets and then passed through a barrier onto the platforms.

"See, I told you," Tomasz whispered and nodded toward the man who was checking the tickets at the barrier.

"Yes, but how do we get past him?" Leo asked.

"We don't go that way! But first, we've got to find the time of the next train to Danzig and which platform it leaves from. Look, there's a list of times over there. You're good at reading—go and see."

Leo checked the timetable carefully, running his finger along the line three times, until he was sure that there was a train to Danzig leaving at eight o'clock from Platform C.

"What time is it now?" Tomasz asked when Leo reported back.

"Just past a quarter till."

"We've got to hurry then. Come on."

They darted back onto the street and sprinted along the front of the station. About a hundred meters down the road, Tomasz stopped and pointed to the fence. "Give me a leg up, and I'll pull you over."

Leo cupped his hands, and Tomasz stepped onto them and

scrambled upward. He straddled the fence and reached down and pulled Leo up to join him. They jumped down on the other side and immediately pressed themselves back against the fence as a train steamed slowly past them into the station.

They crept along the tracks to the rear of the train and then looked down the platform. People were pouring out of the carriages and making their way toward the main hall.

"That's Platform A," Leo said, pointing to the sign. "C must be over there."

They crossed the railway lines, keeping low, and arrived next to the train at Platform C. Tomasz crouched down and crabbed his way under the train toward the platform. Leo followed, praying that its big shiny wheels didn't start to roll and cut them to pieces.

The platform was full of passengers boarding the train. It was impossible to climb up there without being seen, so they crawled back to the other side and looked up. The door handle was high above them.

"Leg up," Tomasz ordered, and Leo cupped his hands again and lifted him as high as he could.

Tomasz reached up for the handle, twisted it, and opened the door.

"What the devil…?" came a voice from inside.

Tomasz slammed the door in shock and fell back to the ground.

"Try the next one," he said, scampering along the track toward the next compartment.

Once more, Leo lifted him, and this time Tomasz stretched up to look through the window first. "It's empty," he said, and then opened the door. He scrambled inside and then reached down and took Leo's outstretched hand.

"Hey, you!" someone cried. Leo glanced toward the main concourse and saw two railway workers pointing at him. Tomasz hauled him upward and he stumbled into the compartment.

"Someone saw us," Leo said, dashing across the carriage to the other door. He pulled the window down and looked out toward the concourse. The big clock was pointing to eight. The stationmaster was waving a green flag. Suddenly, the train jolted as a huge plume of steam shot out from the side of the engine and the wheels began to turn.

"We're going!" Tomasz cried excitedly, squashing Leo so he could lean out of the window too.

There was a jerk as the engine's wheels spun for a moment on the rails. Then smoke puffed out of the funnel, the wheels gripped, and the train started to reverse out of the station. Leo's heart lifted with hope.

Suddenly a figure burst through the cloud of steam wafting across the platform. It was one of the railway workers. He ran toward the stationmaster, shouting and pointing. When the stationmaster heard the cries, he lowered his green flag, grabbed a red flag from his belt, and started along the platform, waving it wildly to catch the driver's attention.

"Don't let him see it. Don't let him see it," Leo begged under his breath.

The train was gathering speed and, for a moment, Leo thought his prayer had been answered. Then the stationmaster drew level with the driver's cab, and a second later, there was a screech of metal as the train lurched to a stop.

People poked their heads out of the windows to see what was happening as the stationmaster and the railway worker came running along the platform. Leo and Tomasz sped across to the other door but the second railway worker was standing on the tracks outside the carriage, blocking their escape.

Tomasz sat down on the seat and pulled Leo down next to him.

"I'll do the talking," he said just before the door opened and the stationmaster stepped into the carriage.

"You two! Out of here!" the man ordered.

"What do you mean? We're going to Danzig," Tomasz protested.

"Oh, are you? And where are your tickets?"

"We're getting them at the other end," Tomasz said calmly. "My father's waiting there, and he'll pay when we arrive. That's what we always do. He's a count, you see, and he's got an arrangement with the railway company."

Tomasz said it with such conviction that, for a moment, the stationmaster hesitated. Then Leo saw his eyes flick over their ragged clothes.

"A count, you say?"

"That's right," Tomasz said, with a broad smile that showed his missing front teeth.

"Well, I'm King Wilhelm of Prussia," the stationmaster said, grabbing Leo and Tomasz and pulling them to their feet, "and I want you off this train."

He pushed them to the door and onto the platform where the railway worker seized them by their arms and held them fast. The stationmaster closed the carriage door and waved the green flag toward the driver, who disappeared back into his cab, and a moment later, the train started moving again. Leo and Tomasz stood on the platform and watched longingly as it steamed past them, out of the station and away on its journey.

"I can't answer for what my father will do when we don't arrive in Danzig," Tomasz said as the stationmaster came toward them.

"Well, I know what I'll do if you keep on with your lies, you cheeky young snap!" the man said, raising his hand and clipping Tomasz sharply around the head. "I'll call the police and let them deal with you."

"Shhh!" Leo warned, as Tomasz opened his mouth to respond.

"That's right, you tell him," the stationmaster said. "Now listen, I've got a son about your age and I'd hate to see him in jail, which is what'll happen to you if I hand you over to the police. So take my advice: Stay away from this station, and I'll forget all about you. But if I clap eyes on you again, you'll regret it. Understand?"

Leo nodded, and then nudged Tomasz, who reluctantly followed suit.

"Good!" the stationmaster went on. "Now, I'm going to turn my back and count to twenty. And when I look around I don't want to see hide nor hair of you. One…Two…"

The railway worker let them go, and they belted away down the platform, past the ticket barrier, across the main hall, and out onto the street.

"Your tongue will get us hanged!" Leo growled when they slowed down outside the station.

"He nearly believed me," Tomasz grinned, and then laughed as Leo cuffed him.

Leo glanced around nervously. Here they were, back on the streets of Bromberg, with the possibility of bumping into Borys at any minute. They had to find somewhere safe for the night, and the nearest place was the tramps' shelter under the overhang. He suggested it to Tomasz, and they trotted along to the end of the road and started along the path through the woods.

"The railway's on the other side of this, isn't it?" Tomasz said, pointing to the fence they were skirting.

"Don't you dare!" Leo snapped, as Tomasz leaned against the wood and peered through the cracks.

"Just looking. Hey!"

"What?" Leo asked, pressing his eye to one of the cracks.

"There's a goods train."

"So?"

"The doors are open. Look. There won't be any passengers or conductors to worry about. All we have to do is sneak on, hide behind the goods, and then jump out at the other end."

"I'm not going to get caught by that stationmaster. You heard what he said. We'll end up in jail."

"He's not going to be watching a goods train, is he? Nobody'll see us. Come on."

Without waiting for a reply, Tomasz scrambled up and over the fence.

"Come on," he whispered hoarsely from the other side.

But Leo hesitated. Surely there was some other way to get away from Borys. They could walk out of Bromberg. They could walk all the way to Danzig, if necessary. Why risk getting caught?

"Tom, listen…" he called.

"Are you coming or not?" Tomasz hissed.

"Wait a minute. We could—"

"I'm going. 'Bye."

"Tom?"

Silence.

Still, Leo hesitated. He peeped through the crack again. There was no sign of Tomasz. He was already gone.

A jag of fear shot through him, and he grabbed the top of the fence and pulled himself up and over. As he landed on the other side, Tomasz stepped out of the shadows and smiled teasingly. "Thought I'd gone, didn't you?"

Leo nodded. Despite his anger at being fooled, he smiled with relief.

"Idiot!" Tomasz chuckled, giving him a playful punch on the

arm. "I'm not going to America without my best friend, am I? Come on. Let's get on that train."

It was as easy as Tomasz had predicted. They dashed across the tracks and hauled themselves up into the goods train. They found themselves in a wagon piled high with sacks of grain and managed to squeeze into a comfortable gap behind them, well hidden from prying eyes.

Half an hour later, they heard someone coming along the train and closing the doors. They held their breath, but their door slid smoothly along and slammed into place without a problem. Not long afterward, the train lurched and they began to move.

"Tomorrow, we'll be in Danzig," Tomasz said, groping for Leo's hand in the darkness and shaking it.

They lay back against the sacks and listened to the rattling and creaking of the train as it rolled away from Bromberg. Leo closed his eyes and was slipping into sleep when the train stopped. There were voices, somewhere ahead near the engine. They strained their ears, trying to hear what was being said. Were they searching the train? After a couple of minutes, the voices stopped, and they heard a hiss of steam and the squeak of wheels as the engine started again.

But they weren't moving.

The noise of the engine grew fainter and fainter, until it finally faded away entirely. It had gone. They had been left behind.

They crept out from their hiding place and went over to the door. They grabbed one of the struts and pulled, but the door didn't move.

It was bolted from the outside.

Chapter 19

THE THIRST WAS WORSE THAN THE HUNGER.

When the sun came up the next morning, the wood of the wagon absorbed the heat, and the temperature inside rose steadily until sweat was pouring off them. On top of that, the air was filled with dust from the grain—they could see it floating in the lines of sunlight that streamed through some cracks in the wagon walls—and it tickled their throats and lungs.

They roasted and they coughed and they longed for water.

Sometimes they pressed up against the small gaps between the slats of the wagon's walls, trying to breathe fresh air, and hoping to see someone outside who would free them from the fiery heat. But all they saw were rows and rows of other wagons on parallel railway lines, seemingly abandoned. Once they heard a steam engine arrive nearby. They yelled and yelled, hoping to be heard above the clanking noises as the engine was attached to some wagons, but the train eventually puffed away, and silence descended again.

"It'll be us next time," Leo said. "We'll be all right."

Tomasz smiled, and then started singing:

"There's a train on the track, a train on the track.
We're going away and we're not coming back.
Leo and Tomasz are—"

He stopped as a wracking cough shook his whole frame.

Night fell, and the heat dissipated as quickly as it had built up.

Soon they found themselves shivering, and they pressed against each other in the little space behind the sacks, trying to keep warm. They awoke at early dawn as another steam train chugged by in the distance, but it didn't stop, and the brief hope of rescue faded.

Hunger gnawed at them. Tomasz pulled out his knife and made a slit in one of the sacks, but the grain was dry and difficult to chew and swallow, especially as their tongues were thick and swollen. They gave up trying to eat it.

They dozed throughout the day, as the heat made their eyelids heavy, and the dry dustiness made it hard to breathe.

Leo dreamed of the meadows down by the River Netze. He saw himself there with his brother, Alexsy, catching crayfish in the deep pools. He knelt by the edge of one of the pools and sipped the cool, clear water. His tongue stuck to the roof of his mouth as he tried to swallow. He woke up to the burning heat and found that his eyes were so gummed up, he could hardly open them. Tomasz lay next to him, his mouth open and a strange rasping noise coming from his throat.

Leo nudged him awake, and Tomasz peered round, trying to work out where he was.

"Thirsty," he finally said.

"Me too," Leo said.

At long last, the cool of night fell, and with it came a burst of energy. Tomasz decided that they would have to break their way out of the wagon. They began kicking and pounding the slats, hoping to split them, but they ended up with nothing more than sore fists and feet. Then Tomasz took out his knife and tried to pry one of the slats away from the struts, but he was worried that the blade might snap, so he tried whittling the edge of one of the slats instead.

"It's no use. The blade's getting blunt!" he said after about half an hour—during which he had sliced away only a few centimeters of the wood. "We'll be dead before I can make a hole big enough to squeeze through."

It was dark now inside the wagon. Leo couldn't see Tomasz's expression, but he could hear the despair in his voice and, for the first time, he began to be scared. He had told himself that their wagon was bound to be moved soon, but now he realized that perhaps it wouldn't happen for a week, perhaps two. Without food, and especially without water, they really might die. He heard Tomasz slump back against the sacks and drop to the floor with a deep, hopeless sigh.

Leo sat next to his friend, not knowing what to do or say, but just listening to the creaks of the wood as the night air cooled it. Then, in the darkness, Tomasz spoke.

"I'm being punished." His voice was cracked, and the dryness of his mouth made the words so thick and slurred that Leo thought he'd misheard him. There was a long silence. Then Tomasz spoke again. "God is punishing me."

"Don't be stupid," Leo said, trying to sound light-hearted.

"I killed someone."

"Oh, come on, Tom. Stop making things up."

"I did!" Tomasz said urgently, suddenly swinging around and grabbing hold of Leo. "I did! It wasn't my fault, but I killed him."

"Who?"

"He tried to kill me."

"Who? Why?" Leo asked, confused

"Because of the silver coins."

"What?" Leo said, trying to wrestle free from Tomasz's grip. "What silver coins? Tom, you're hurting my arm!"

Tomasz let go of Leo's arm and sat back.

"What are you going on about?" Leo asked.

"You don't believe me, but it's true. My mother lied to me. My father wasn't my father, but he loved me, and my father wanted me gone."

"What's that got to do with silver coins? You're talking in riddles," Leo said, wondering if the heat was making Tomasz delirious.

"Oh, my father loved riddles," Tomasz said, changing direction again. "He used to tell them to me while I helped him in the shop. Riddle me this: 'My fortress walls are marble white, there's a crystal stream within. I have no doors or windows, but thieves steal gold when they break in.' What am I?"

"I know that one. It's an egg," Leo said, trying to humor him.

"Yes!" Tomasz croaked excitedly, and then broke into a fit of coughing.

There was a rattle of phlegm in his throat, but he coughed once more and, when he spoke again, his voice was clear. He seemed calm as he started telling his story.

Chapter 20

I WAS ALWAYS IN THE SHOP WITH MY FATHER WHEN I WAS GROWING up," Tomasz began. "My mother used to say, 'He needs to learn more than shoes and boots,' and my father always nodded and promised to send me to learn my letters one day.

"But I was his only child, and I came along when he had given up all hope of having a son to love. So he wanted me with him all the time, even when I was too young to do more than sit at his feet and play with the scraps of leather that fell on the floor. And later, when he taught me his trade, he was proud because I had nimble fingers, and he said I would be a finer cobbler than him one day. 'What need of letters then?' he used to whisper to me, looking toward the kitchen door in case my mother heard.

"He's an old man, Leo—thirty years older than my mother—but what a man…Oh, you'd like him, and he'd like you. We laughed all the time. He was so…kind…and loving…"

There was a pause, and in the dark, Leo could just make out Tomasz swiftly wiping his eyes.

"My mother loves me too, I know that. But she lied to me all those years. She hid it from me. But I mustn't speak ill of her. She thought she was doing right. And for thirteen years, I was happy. Really happy. We didn't have much, but we had love…and we were always laughing and smiling."

Tomasz paused, as if lost in the sunny memories. Leo held his tongue, though he longed to ask questions. At last, Tomasz went on.

"And then it all ended. I guessed something was wrong. There were whispers in the house. Strange glances between them. My father was quieter in the workshop—no songs, no riddles, no laughter. I asked him if he was displeased with me or if he was ill, but he just shook his head and quickly bent to his work again. Then sometimes, I caught him looking at me. What was it in his eyes? Longing? Fear?

"Then one morning, my mother announced that I had to go with her to the great house on the Schuvin estate, because the count had ordered some boots, and we needed to take his measurements. I didn't suspect anything, so I got ready and opened the workshop door to say good-bye to my father.

"He didn't look up from his work. He only mumbled something I couldn't hear. Then, suddenly, he dropped his hammer, ran over, and held me and kissed me. I felt his tears on my cheek. He sobbed and said he loved me, and I wasn't to forget him. I couldn't understand what he meant. But my mother was pulling at my hand, saying he was a silly old man to cry like that, because I would be coming back that evening. And I believed I would."

Tomasz was breathing hard, fighting back tears, and he had to pause before he could go on.

"It's a long walk to Schuvin, and my mother didn't say a word until we passed through the big gates and started up the drive toward the count's house. There was a sudden downpour, and she took my hand and pulled me under a tree. And there, pressed up against the trunk, she told me. We weren't there to measure for boots…

"The words poured out of her—all the secrets she'd hidden from me.

"My father wasn't my father.

"She had worked here, in this very house at Schuvin, when she was fifteen. The son of the count had been twenty at the time, and handsome. He had courted her in secret and had won her heart. But when she fell pregnant, he said he could never marry her, a Jewess from a poor family. He told her she would have to leave, but that he would be generous and would help her. He took her to the village and introduced her to the cobbler, a kind and gentle man who had always longed for a child. He agreed to marry her and pretend he was the father of the baby. Me.

"I heard all this news while the rain dripped down on us. I shivered with the cold and the shock. My mind whirled. I am not a Christian. I am a Jew. I am not the son of a cobbler. I am the son of a count. Everything I thought I was, was a lie.

"We were soaked under that tree, my mother and I. Then we went into this grand house and stood in the hall like drenched dogs, dripping onto the floor. We were led by a servant into the main room, and we stood dripping onto another floor, as my father looked up from his newspaper.

"He stared at me for a long time, and then he finally asked, 'He knows?' My mother nodded. 'Tomasz is his name?' My mother nodded. 'Step forward, Tomasz.'

"I obeyed and stood there while the rain seeped from my clothes and formed a pool under my feet as if I was pissing myself.

"'You will have heard that my father died earlier this year,' he said, and I nodded. 'So I am the Count now. A position of respect and great responsibility…I am going to marry next month, Tomasz…And I hope to have children…A son, God willing…A son who will inherit my name and my estate when I die…You see the problem?'

"I shook my head, because I truly didn't see the problem.

"'You are the problem. I cannot have another son, living so near. Born out of wedlock. And a Jew.'

"I remember how his lip twisted when he said that word—'Jew'—and I realized that this was the new me, Tomasz the Jew.

"'My wife, my future son and heir—I must protect them from scandal,' he said. 'So I need you gone. Away. Far from here. I have made provision. A man is waiting out in the yard. He is leaving today for Berlin. I have paid him to take you with him. You will not go away empty-handed. I will give you money—silver coins from Koln.'

"He took a velvet purse from the desk behind him and handed it to me. It was heavy, and the coins chinked inside.

"'I don't want it,' I said, holding the purse out to him. 'I want to stay with my fa—with the cobbler and my mother.'

"'I cannot permit that. Take the money and go. If you stay, or if I ever hear of you coming back to this area, I shall make sure that your mother and the cobbler lose their house and their living. Look at your mother, Tomasz. She knows that I can and will do that.'

"I turned, and my mother's face was white with fear and grief. She had her hand over her mouth to stop her sobs, and tears were racing down her face. She nodded at me.

"'I have been generous with the money,' the Count went on. 'In the purse, there is the name of a friend I can trust completely. You will give the money to him. He will find you an apprenticeship with a cobbler in Berlin, and he will invest the money, so one day you will be able to set up on your own, as befits a child of my blood.'

"He clicked his fingers. A servant stepped from behind a screen near the door and came and took my arm.

"'Bid farewell to your mother,' the Count said. 'Then my man will take you outside, and your grand new life will begin.'

"The servant turned me around and walked me to my mother. We looked at each other, she and I, unable to speak. Then she took my hand and kissed it. I reached out to hold her, but the servant pulled me away and led me out the door.

"Along a corridor.

"Down a flight of winding stone stairs to the kitchen.

"Across the kitchen, while the cook and her two helpers stared at me.

"Out into the rain. Across the cobbles of the yard to the waiting horse and cart.

"There was a rough canvas roof over the cart, and the servant bundled me under it. I heard him say something to the driver, and the cart began to move.

"I lay on the floor and listened to the creak of the wheels and the clop of the horse's hooves. I held on to the purse.

"And I didn't feel anything. I was numb."

Tomasz's voice was cold and flat, as if that numbness had come back to him. He coughed slightly, and then he was silent.

Chapter 21

LEO SHIVERED AS HE PICTURED TOMASZ LYING ON THE FLOOR OF that cart as it rocked and jolted him away from everything he knew and loved.

The silence went on and on, and Leo almost jumped when Tomasz's voice started up again in the darkness.

"We traveled for five days, and it rained for four of them. All I saw out of the back of the cart were muddy roads and the dark, wet pine trees that pressed in on both sides. The driver hardly spoke to me. At night when we stopped, he gave me food and climbed into the cart to sleep. On the fifth morning, I opened my eyes and saw him staring at the velvet purse I was still gripping in my hand.

"The weather was fine that day, and he told me to sit up front with him while he drove the horse. He chatted away, telling me that his name was Gustaw Neumann and that he made his living by hauling goods from one town to another. 'This is the first time I've had a boy as a cargo,' he said with a laugh. 'A boy with money too. You'll have to be careful in Berlin—thieves on every corner. But I'll see you right. That's what I promised the Count. What are you to him?'

"'Nothing,' I replied.

"'Well, you must be something, for him to go to all this trouble—money and passage to Berlin.'

"'He hates me and never wants to see me again.'

"'Never wants to see you again, eh? Poor you.'

"At the end of the day, we pulled off down a narrow track, and I asked him why we weren't stopping by the side of the road as usual.

"'Don't want prying eyes, do we?' he said. 'Want to keep you safe, like the Count told me.'

"We stopped in a small glade and got down from the cart. The horse began to graze on the grass, and I stood and held his reins and stroked him while the man went to the back of the cart to fetch the bread for our supper. I heard him come back, and when I turned around, he had a knife in his hand, but no bread. He stepped toward me, and I knew he was going to kill me. He drew the knife back to strike, but I whipped the reins and caught him across the face. It was a fierce slap, and when he staggered back in shock, I slipped under the horse and ran for my life.

"I burst through the ferns onto the track and sprinted toward the road. I was nearly there when I glanced over my shoulder to see where Neumann was and my foot caught something on the path. I went sprawling to the ground and twisted my ankle. I scrambled to my feet and tried to run, but the pain was terrible, and I knew he would catch me. I saw a heavy stick on the ground, picked it up, and then turned to defend myself.

"Neumann stopped a short way from me and grinned.

"'I just want the money,' he said, pointing to the pocket where I'd put the purse. 'Give it to me, and I'll let you go. I promise.'

"But I knew he was lying.

"He took a step forward, and I swung the stick. It hit his hand and the knife flew out of his grasp and landed near me. I bent to snatch it up, but he caught me by the hair, pulled my head back, and punched me in the mouth, knocking my teeth out. I went reeling to the ground, and he grabbed the knife and came toward me. I saw him raise it and point it at my chest, and I knew he was going to dive forward and kill me. So I pulled the purse from my pocket and hurled it away, over his head.

"And he stopped. The greedy fool stopped.

"He turned and watched as the purse hit the ground and the coins spilled out into the mud. He let out a little cry and took a couple of paces toward them, and then he hesitated and started to turn back to deal with me.

"Too late. I was already on my feet and had picked up the stick.

"As he spun around, I smashed it against the back of his head, and he collapsed like a poleaxed bullock. The blow snapped the stick in two, and I was sure I had knocked him out, but a second later, he groaned and staggered to his feet.

"A red stain was spreading across his shirt, and the knife was sticking out of his guts. I was too shocked to move, so I just stood there as he stumbled toward me. He grabbed me by the throat and began to squeeze. I raised my hand to try to break his grip, and it banged against the knife. He grunted with pain, but he went on squeezing, so I snatched the handle of the knife and pulled.

"He screamed as the knife slid out, and then he stepped back and looked down at the blood gushing from the wound. His face, it was…twisted…with fury and pain, and he…he started to come toward me again, so I held out the knife to stop him. But he kept coming. Kept coming. He reached for my throat, so I drove the knife forward with all my might. I felt it crunch through his ribs. A second later, I pulled it out, and he crashed backward and lay still. I'd killed him, Leo. I'd killed him."

"It wasn't your fault," Leo said.

"But you know what? I'd killed him, and I didn't care. I was so calm. I wiped the blood off the knife and saw his initials, G.N., on the handle. But I didn't throw it away. I closed it and put it in my pocket. I felt so calm. I picked up the coins and put them back in the purse. Calm.

"I went back to the glade and unhitched the horse from the cart. Calmly. No rush. I tried to get up on the horse's back, but he bucked and kicked. So I left him. I was glad he was free so he could graze in the woods and not starve. Then I walked along the track and pulled the man into the bushes. I felt nothing as I covered him with branches. Nothing.

"I walked out of the woods and back the way we'd come. I couldn't go home, of course, because of what the count had threatened to do to my mother and the cobbler, but I couldn't go to Berlin either. If someone found Neumann's body, that would be the first place the police would look for me. So I wandered. Anywhere. I didn't care.

"It was autumn, and there were berries and fruit and nuts to eat. I lived in the woods until the first frost, and then I began sleeping in barns along the way, stealing food from the farms and moving on every day. I made up songs to keep me happy. I didn't let myself think about home. I didn't let myself think about what I had done to Neumann. I just kept moving.

"I spent the winter in Posen—only forty kilometers from my village—but I never saw anyone I knew. I found little jobs. I stole things. Sometimes, kind people took me in for the night and fed me.

"And then, when spring came, I suddenly started to have dreams about Neumann. I saw him…and animals had been eating him. His face was eaten, but his eyes were staring at me. I wasn't calm anymore. I couldn't stop thinking about what I'd done. I was scared—scared of what I'd done. Scared the police would find me. So I knew I had to go away…far away. I thought of America. I

walked to…Bromberg and…and met you. And now…here I am…
and this…is…my punishment."

Tomasz's voice had become weaker and weaker toward the
end of his story, and now, as if the telling had exhausted him, he
slumped against Leo's shoulder and instantly fell asleep.

Chapter 22

THE THIRD DAY OF HEAT ROASTED THEM AND THE NIGHT chilled them.

On the fourth morning of their captivity, Tomasz didn't wake up.

Leo floated into consciousness and was aware of the pain from his cracked lips and tongue. He rolled over and tried to open his eyes, but he couldn't. His lashes were stuck together, and even when he eased them apart with his fingers, his eyelids barely separated and he peered out at the world through hazy slits.

Tomasz was lying next to him, and he shook him and called his name, but there was no movement. He leaned across and put his ear against his friend's chest. He heard a heartbeat—slow and faint, but still there.

"Wake up," he murmured, pinching the skin on Tomasz's hand, but there was no reaction.

Leo rolled back and stared at the streams of sunlight coming through the wagon's walls, baking the air. He knew he was on the train, but he felt that if he could turn his head, he would find that his mother was there. He tried to move, but his eyes closed, and he slipped away back into darkness.

Dorota was running across the fields near the house. Mama was putting the washing on the line. It was very windy, and sometimes, he could see Dorota, and sometimes, she was hidden behind the clothes. Dorota had something to give him. What was it? Oh yes, she had run down to the stream to fetch water. He was thirsty. Now she was next to him. There was water in her cupped hands, and he thought that there wouldn't be enough, but when he bent to drink, he saw that it was as deep as one of the pools. He sipped at the water, and then realized that someone else wanted to drink—his little brother, Jozef. Poor Jozef needed it more than him. Jozef was coughing and burning with fever.

"Jozef!" he said and his throat was sore—was he catching the cough too? "Come on, Jozef. Be a good boy, and drink up."

He was shaking Jozef because he wouldn't drink, and then he realized that it couldn't be Jozef—he wasn't on the train. He was shaking Tomasz.

But Tomasz wouldn't wake up.

He lay down again. Had Tomasz really killed a man? Or had he dreamed that too, like the dream that Dorota had given him water? It wasn't a dream. Tomasz had told him the story. But was it true? Tomasz was always telling lies. But he had the knife with the initials—G.N. And he'd lost his front teeth. But where was the money? Ah, yes, that was the weak bit in the story. He didn't have money. He was poor. If he'd had money, they could have bought tickets for the train. And something to drink. Oh, for something to drink. Now they were going to die here in this stifling wagon. They were roasting to death. Better to let go and sleep…

From far away, there was a ringing sound, pulling him out of the blackness. The sound was near. The sun had gone down, and it was cooler again in the wagon.

Ring. Clang. Like bells on a church. It couldn't be a church. It was going away. The ring was fainter now. And was someone talking in the distance?

Ring. Ring.

Someone was hitting the wheels of the train. Who? Borys? Jozef? Was his brother being naughty and hitting the train? Papa would take his belt to him if he found out. No, it must be Tomasz, he was the bad one. He'd killed a man. He told lies.

No, Tomasz was here, next to him. Tomasz was cold. Leo took off his waistcoat and was just laying it on his friend when the train jerked and they started to move. Leo made himself stand up to make sure that he wasn't dreaming. He stumbled over to the side of the wagon and peered through one of the slats. The moon was shining, and he could see trees, gray and black, rolling past. They were moving. There was a cottage, with a light in the window. And then the cottage was gone. Yes, they were moving.

Suddenly, he wanted to cry. His eyes pricked, but no water came to them. He couldn't cry. A savage headache began throbbing all the way around his skull. He staggered back to his friend and slumped down next to him. He shook his shoulder, "Tom, we're going. Tom, wake up. We're going…we're going to Danzig. And America."

He tried to hear Tomasz's heartbeat, but the noise of the train was too loud. He put his hand on Tomasz's chest—was it the juddering of the wagon, or was there a slight movement there? He put his cheek close to Tomasz's mouth. Was it the swirl of air in the wagon, or was there a faint stir of breath? He lifted Tomasz and cradled him in his arms as the train rocked and rattled along. He was cold.

Strips of gray light began to show through the slats. It was dawn. He left Tomasz and got up to peer out. It was raining. Drops of water were hitting the side of the wagon, and a fine spray was flying in through the gap. He put his mouth up close to the wood and tried to catch it, but his tongue was so numb he could hardly feel it. He stayed there, sucking in the fresh air and the droplets until at last, his tongue was moist. He tried to swallow, but there wasn't enough to wet the back of his throat, and it made him cough. The coughing doubled the throb of the headache.

The train began to slow, and he was gripped with terror. Would they stop and be left standing for days again? He peeked through the gap. There were houses alongside the track, more and more of them, and houses stretching back behind them. They were coming into a town. Was it Danzig? There was a flash of light on water in a gap between some houses. The sea? Now the train was just creeping along, and there was a platform. It was a station. The train came to a halt. He pressed his eye against the wood and caught a glimpse of a man.

"Help!" he tried to shout, but his throat seized up. Only a whispered croak came out, so he bunched his fists and began pounding on the wood.

There was a noise from outside—the slide of a bolt. Then light burst in as the door swept open.

"What in God's name are you doing? Get out of there," the man said sharply, but then he saw the state Leo was in and spoke more gently. "What's up, lad?"

His eyes followed Leo's pointing finger to where Tomasz was lying motionless.

"Oh, sweet Jesus," the man breathed and climbed up into the wagon. He knelt down next to Tomasz, tapped him lightly on the cheek, and then bent to listen to his chest. He took Tomasz's limp body in his arms and walked back to the door. He laid Tomasz on the floor while he jumped out and helped Leo down. Then he picked Tomasz up again and lifted him up over his shoulder as if he weighed nothing.

"Is he dead?" Leo asked, his voice a hoarse whisper.

"He's in a bad way," the man said.

They walked across the platform and through a door marked Station Crew. The man laid Tomasz on a table and then stood looking at him as if he wasn't sure what to do next.

"Water," Leo croaked.

"Yes, yes—of course," the man said, and reached over for a jug of water that was standing on top of a big pot-bellied stove. "Here, you first."

Leo took the jug and raised it to his lips. Water spilled into his mouth and around the side of his lips, splashing his shirt and dripping on the floor. He knew that he should leave some for Tomasz, but once he had started, he couldn't stop—he gulped and glugged until there was no more.

"I'm sorry," he said, holding out the empty jug.

"Don't worry—I'll get more," the man said, heading for the door.

Leo could feel the cold water, swilling and gurgling down into his stomach. A moment later, he felt it rise up again, and he only just made it to the door before he doubled over and spewed up everything he had drunk. Then, trembling, he fell to his knees in the middle of the puddle he had made. His head was spinning and he felt as if he was going to pass out, until a strong hand grasped him under the arm and raised him to his feet. It was the man.

"You'd better take it more slowly this time," the man said as he half carried him back into the office. He lowered Leo onto a chair and gave him the jug again. "Just a couple of sips to get your belly used to it."

He did as he was told and then handed the jug back. He watched as the man dipped his finger into the water and dripped a couple of drops onto Tomasz's parched lips. The drops ran down the side of Tomasz's chin, but his mouth opened slightly and on the next attempt, the man managed to drip some water inside. They both saw the movement as Tomasz swallowed, and the man smiled and crossed himself. He handed the jug to Leo again.

"Just a few sips. Take it easy."

It took nearly a half hour of sipping and waiting, and sipping and waiting, before Leo felt able to take a big gulp. Like before, once he had started gulping he couldn't stop. But this time, when he finished the jug, there was no rush to puke it up again. Instead, he sat, feeling the water clear his head and give him strength.

"I must get back to work," the man said. "I'll leave you to carry on giving the water to your friend—a little at a time, like I've been doing. Can you do that?"

Leo said yes, but he was astonished at how weak he felt when he tried to stand up and walk. He swayed and had to grab hold of the table to stop himself from keeling over.

"Here, you sit there," the man said, dragging the chair over and sitting Leo on it before he went back to work.

Leo copied what the man had done, dipping his finger in the water and letting it run into Tomasz's mouth. Bit by bit, there were more signs of life. His face was still deathly pale, but the tips of his large ears began to glow pink. Once, his tongue flicked out and licked his lips, and it looked almost as if he smiled briefly. His breathing became stronger, and Leo was thrilled to see the steady rise and fall of his friend's chest.

Finally, he raised Tomasz's head and held the jug to his lips, making sure that the water trickled, rather than flooded, into his mouth. Tomasz gulped, and at the same time, his eyes flickered open. They closed again almost as soon as they had opened, but this time there was no doubt—the edges of his mouth turned upward in a smile. Leo took hold of Tomasz's hand, and he felt an answering squeeze.

After that, the progress was rapid, and with Leo's help, Tomasz got off the table and sat on a chair, although he still had to lean back against the wall to stop his head from lolling all over the place. He couldn't talk properly, but he kept making the same mumbling sound until, at last, Leo realized he was saying, "Danzig?" As soon as the man came back into the office at lunchtime, Leo asked him.

"Danzig? No, this is Thorn," the man said. "If you've come from Bromberg, you're going in the wrong direction. But I don't want to know what you're up to or where you're going. By rights, I should be calling the police and having you two hauled off to jail. Now, look, I've brought you some more water, a bit of bread, and some cooked cabbage. I know you've both been through a lot and you're still weak, but I'll be back in an hour and I don't want to find you here. Understood?"

Leo nodded and said, "Thank you."

The man smiled and winked, and then turned and went out the door.

They ate and drank. Then, with Tomasz holding on to Leo's shoulder for support, they limped out of the station.

Chapter 23

Leo would always think of Thorn as a lucky town. Almost from the moment they left the station, things went right for them. A man saw that Tomasz was having difficulty walking, so he invited them to sit on his empty barrow while he wheeled it down the hill. They rattled over the old wooden bridge across the river and into the town. On the way, they told the man what had happened to them and when he heard they had nowhere to sleep, he invited them to stay with his family for the night.

He lived in a small house with his wife, their four young children, and his old mother. It was down near the River Weichsel—although he kept calling it the River Wisła because, he said, that was the proper old Polish name that his father and his grandfather and his great-grandfather, and all his ancestors had used.

"I'm damned if I'll call it something else because the damned Prussians say so. It's always been the Wisła, and it'll be the Wisła when we drive the tyrant out of our country. And then we can start calling our town by its proper name too. It's Toruń, not Thorn."

"Shush, Stanislaw," his mother said, looking nervously at the door. "If someone hears you—"

"Who's to hear? Besides, I fear no man, especially not a Prussian."

"Aye, and you should remember that 'Never-Fear' was eaten by the wolves," his mother said.

"Better to be eaten by wolves than see our poor country eaten by worms. While she's ruled by the Prussians and Russians and Austrians, that's all she is—a corpse eaten by worms. But one day we'll rise up and rid our homeland of these invaders."

"Stanislaw, that's enough talk of worms and corpses just before bedtime," his wife said. "The children won't sleep."

She took the four youngsters up to the bedroom, and a short while later, Stanislaw's mother followed them.

"Good night," Leo and Tomasz called as she slowly climbed the stairs, but the old lady didn't reply.

"Ah, she's sulking because she usually sleeps down here in her chair next to the fireplace," Stanislaw chuckled. "But she thinks it wouldn't be seemly to sleep in the same room as two strange young men. Isn't that right, Mother?"

The old lady snorted and continued her slow progress up the stairs.

"But where will she sleep?" Leo asked

"Oh, there's room on our mattress tonight, although it will be mighty crowded with the four little ones and me and my wife. One night won't do any harm, but you'll understand that I can't let you stay longer."

The following morning, before dawn, Stanislaw woke Leo and Tomasz from their deep sleep, and they followed him out into the dark streets and helped him pull his cart to the market. He bought them each a mug of soup from a café where all the traders were having breakfast, and he asked around to see if any of them wanted to hire two young helpers. None of them did.

"There's not much work around at the moment. Everyone's worried about this war that's supposed to be coming. That, and the cholera."

"Cholera?" Leo asked, feeling a chill sweep through his body.

"Yes, there were twenty cases in the city last week. A doctor at the university says the disease is in the river, so people are in a panic. So you be careful where you drink water—do you hear?"

"Don't worry," Leo said. "We'll only be here for a day or so, until Tomasz feels stronger. Then we'll set off to Danzig again. May God repay you for your kindness."

"God will repay me the day when Poland is free," Stanislaw said, smiling. "Well, I'd best get on. Farewell, my young friends."

He shook their hands and then trundled his cart away into the gray dawn.

They wandered through the streets, and Leo was amazed by how quickly Tomasz got used to this new town—"No, no, Leo, not down that lane—it leads back to the river. We need to go toward that church spire. That'll be where the shops are."

He was still weak, though, and when they got to the church, he had to sit on the steps to get his strength back. A coach drawn by two white horses clattered along the road and stopped near them. A woman climbed out, and as she passed them on her way into the church, she dropped a coin in Tomasz's lap.

"One rotten pfennig? Bah. The mean cat!" he hissed, looking at the coin. "She needn't think that God's going to bless her for giving measly charity like that."

"It'll buy us a bit of bread," Leo said, and then added sarcastically, "Besides, you don't need money—you've got all those silver coins your father, the count, gave you."

"That's for America."

"Oh, yes?" Leo laughed. "Mr. Bulge-Pockets, who's got all this money but sleeps in the streets and begs for food."

"I told you. It's for America," Tomasz protested. "We don't want to arrive with nothing, do we?"

"So where is it then, this fortune?"

"Aha!" Tomasz said, tapping the side of his nose. "It's hidden."

"Where? Up your ass?" Leo laughed, and after a second, Tomasz joined in. As usual, it was impossible to upset him.

They were looking for a baker's shop to buy some bread when Tomasz nudged him, indicating a fat man sitting on a chair on the pavement across the road.

"I smell work. Look at the shop, and look at his hand."

It was a cobbler shop, and the man had a large bandage wrapped around his left hand.

"I do the talking," Tomasz whispered as he pulled Leo across the road and stopped in front of the man. "Good morning, Master Cobbler."

"I'm not interested," the man said grumpily, the smell of vodka rising off his breath.

"Let me guess—a blow from the hammer, and your finger's gone septic," Tomasz said.

"Not just the damn finger—it's the whole hand," the cobbler said, wincing as he raised it.

"You were working with leather fresh from the tannery."

"Yes! How did you know?"

"It happened to my father—twice," Tomasz replied. "That fresh tanned leather is a devil for sending cuts septic. I had to run the whole shop on my own while my father was getting well. Luckily, I've got nimble fingers, and he'd schooled me well in the trade. Otherwise, we'd have near starved to death. His hand took a month to heal."

"Don't tell me—I've been off for seventeen days already. So your father's a cobbler, eh?"

"One of the best, and he taught me everything he knows. Oh,

well, must be getting on. Good day to you, Master Cobbler," Tomasz said, taking Leo's arm and turning away.

"Hold a minute, hold a minute," the cobbler said. "You're not looking for work, are you?"

"Could be, could be," Tomasz said. "My friend and I are new to town, so we might be willing to work in return for lodgings and food and a fair cut of the takings."

"Your friend too?" the cobbler asked, looking dubiously at Leo.

"He's my apprentice. New to the trade, but willing, very willing," Tomasz said, slapping Leo on the back.

The man still seemed to be hesitating, but Tomasz pointed to his calfskin belt and said, "If you doubt my skill, look at the stitching I did on my belt. It's fine, isn't it?"

The man peered at the belt and then drew back, nodding, "Very fine, indeed." He held out his right hand. "Plinski's the name. I'll give food and lodgings to both of you, guaranteed. And a small cut on the takings—five percent."

"Ten," Tomasz said.

"Five—no higher," Mr. Plinski said.

"Twenty," Tomasz said, and Mr. Plinski's eyes widened in surprise.

"What? All right, seven," he said, and Tomasz took the proffered hand and shook it.

Chapter 24

APART FROM MEAL TIMES, WHEN THEY WENT UP THE DARK STAIRS to Mr. and Mrs. Plinski's kitchen to eat, Leo and Tomasz spent all their time in the workshop. They worked there and slept there, making their beds on the large batches of hides under the workbench. Leo felt he would never get the smell of leather out of his nostrils.

At dawn they were up and at work, Tomasz seated on a stool at the bench and Leo by his side, handing him the materials and the tools as they were needed for the various jobs. Leo quickly learned the names of the various hammers Tomasz called for and the different-sized awls needed to punch holes in the leather. He learned how to grease a thread with beeswax and slip it through the eye of a needle ready for sewing. He anticipated the moment Tomasz would need a knife, a hole punch, a nipper, or the brass nails. He did some of the work himself, using the skiving knife to thin the leather at the seams for easier sewing.

"We'll make a cobbler of you yet," Tomasz kept telling him, and Leo was pleased when Tomasz was pleased with him.

On the other hand, Leo hated it when Mr. Plinski stood behind him, watching his work. It made him clumsy, and he always dropped things or made mistakes, while the cobbler sighed or clicked his tongue in annoyance.

Plinski could even make Tomasz nervous until finally he

told the cobbler that they wouldn't work if he came into the workshop.

"See what the young people are like nowadays," Mr. Plinski grumbled. "Hot-headed, sure of themselves, rude to their elders, and deaf to words of wisdom."

"Think what you like," Tomasz said. "I can't work with you here. And if I can't work, none of us eats—so off with you. And by the way, you ought to change your tanner—these batches are not in the same class as the leather my father uses."

"Change the tanner I've used all my life? Listen to him," Plinski raged. "From the young, we're supposed to learn our jobs these days. From the young!"

But when Tomasz laid down the boots he was repairing and folded his arms defiantly, Plinski stopped complaining and went upstairs.

Then the work began again, twice as fast, and twice as efficiently, while Tomasz told stories that made Leo laugh, or sang old songs, often making up new words:

"Cobbler Tomasz, mend my shoe
Get it done by half past two.
When Plinski does it, it's too late
It's never done till half past eight."

When they finished work each day, they would spend half an hour secretly working on a pair of boots Tomasz had decided to make for Leo.

"We'll probably have to do a lot of walking, and your sandals are falling to pieces," he pointed out. "Besides, old Plinski isn't paying us enough—we've only earned three silbergroschen for all those shoes we've repaired—so he owes us a bit of leather and thread."

One evening they went upstairs for the evening meal and found that Mr. Plinski had taken the bandage off his hand. His fingers were still red and swollen and three of his nails had gone black, but it was obvious that the infection had gone from the wound.

"Went to see the wise woman," Mr. Plinski said. "She used a white-hot knife to cut me open, and then she drained the poison and rubbed a potion on it. Stung like a dozen bees, it did, but she says I'll be back at work within the week. Now that's a good reason for a cup of vodka."

"Huh, as if you need a reason," Mrs. Plinski said bitterly as he filled a cup and drank it. "It was the vodka that caused your injury in the first place. Drunken old fool."

"Where's your respect, woman? No wonder the world goes wrong, when women speak to their husbands like that!" Mr. Plinski roared. "I'm the one who puts the food on the table."

"It's these lads who put the food on the table," Mrs. Plinski snapped, and Leo and Tomasz kept their eyes down, hoping that the cobbler wouldn't react and pick on them.

"Yes, they're good lads," they were surprised to hear him say, but they realized why when he added, "Not like our two boys, damn them!"

Hardly a meal went by without Mr. Plinski attacking their two sons, and Mrs. Plinski defending them.

"How can you speak so?" Mrs. Plinski cried, outraged.

"You ruined them, that's why," Mr. Plinski grumbled, pouring another cup of vodka and downing it. "They're like all the young today—no respect, no discipline, no obedience to their elders. It's all your fault. You spoiled them, and they're rotten to the core."

"His own children!" Mrs. Plinski sniffed, raising her apron to wipe her eyes. "He speaks ill of his own children when they're fighting for the honor of their country."

"Honor of the country, my ass! They only joined the army so they could strut around in their uniforms like peacocks. And you encouraged them so you could boast to your friends—'Oh, my soldier boys, they're so brave!' Huh. They won't be so brave when it comes to fighting. They'll be messing their breeches, like as not. I could have gotten them off military service. All I had to do was ask my friend, the mayor. But you wouldn't have it. Well, you'll be sorry if this war starts and they stop a French bullet."

"Listen to him, Lord, listen to him! Wishing death on his own sons," Mrs. Plinski cried.

Mr. Plinski took another cupful of vodka, and sweat began to break out on his fat red face. "Oh, stop whining and bring our food!" he ordered.

Mrs. Plinksi got to her feet and slowly walked over to the stove. She picked up the big pot of stew and turned around. "You want food?" she sobbed. "Well, there it is. Eat it like the pig you are!" With that, she tipped the contents of the pot onto the floor.

There was an astonished silence, and then Mr. Plinski banged his fists on the table. An instant later, he leaped up, howling and nursing his injured hand.

Leo nudged Tomasz and, even though they hadn't eaten, they got up and went downstairs while Mr. and Mrs. Plinski continued to scream insults at each other.

"I tell you what," Tomasz said when they were back down in the workshop. "You go out and buy us something to eat, while I finish your boots. I need to stretch them a bit on the last and dubbin them to make them waterproof."

"What's the rush?"

"Well," Tomasz said, lowering his voice, "I'm fed up working for next to nothing, with Fatgut Plinski always breathing down my neck. And them always scrapping like cats and dogs. Then there's all this talk of cholera in the city. I think it's time to get moving again. What about you?"

Leo nodded, and Tomasz winked and gave him a grin.

Late that evening, after they'd eaten, Tomasz took the boots off the last. Leo had seen them being made—had even helped trim some of the leather himself—but his throat suddenly tightened as his friend handed him the gift. They were the first proper shoes he'd had in his life and, as he looked at them gleaming in the candle-light, tears came to his eyes.

"Do you like them?" Tomasz asked.

Leo nodded, not trusting himself to speak.

The next morning, while it was still dark, they slipped the catch on the front door and let themselves out onto the cool, empty street. They hurried to the corner, and then Tomasz stopped and pointed to the boots that Leo was carrying.

"Why aren't you wearing them? Don't you like them?"

"Of course I like them. They're…perfect."

"So why don't you put them on?" Tomasz asked.

"Look at the street. They'll get dirty."

Tomasz burst out laughing, and a moment later, Leo saw the joke and joined in. He put the boots on the ground and slipped his feet into them. They fit perfectly. Then, arm in arm, still laughing, he and Tomasz turned the corner and started their journey out of town.

Chapter 25

Tomasz was all for trekking across country but in the end, they agreed to follow the river.

"This way, we can't get lost," Leo reasoned. "A soldier told me it goes all the way down to Danzig."

"Yes, and we might get there in about six months," Tomasz joked.

They followed a track that ran parallel to the river. The waters were rushing high and fast, and there were signs of recent flooding—huge puddles on the track, bits of wood and rubbish stranded in bushes, and two drowned sheep, whose bloated bodies were crawling with maggots. Clouds of mosquitoes hovered in the warm, moist air.

By the time they stopped for the night in a barn outside the small village of Gurske, Leo's feet were hurting. He had blisters around his ankles, where the top of the boots had chafed the skin.

"You'll get used to them. They'll wear into your shape in a couple of days," Tomasz assured him. It was true. At the end of the second day, they hurt less than the first day.

They lay down for that second night in a woodshed on the grounds of a large, isolated house that looked unoccupied. A short distance from the woodshed was a tall pole with a cartwheel nailed to the top. A stork had built its nest up there, and just before dusk, the big bird flew back to the nest and stood there, unmoving, as the light faded to night. It made Leo think of the pole Papa had built. Were the storks still there? Had they brought some luck to the family?

He closed his eyes and thought of them all. Perhaps they were thinking of him too. Was Mama sitting near the fireplace, seeing him in her mind's eye? Was Alexsy lying on the mattress with Jozef and Stefan, whispering about him and wondering where he was? Or had they all forgotten him?

Leo half woke in the middle of the night, dimly aware that something was pressing against his leg. He thought that it must be Tomasz huddling for warmth, and then he drifted back into sleep. But in the morning, when he opened his eyes, he saw that a dog had snuggled between him and Tomasz. The dog wagged her tail as Leo sat up, and then she rolled over on her back and lay there with her mouth open, begging for a caress.

"Hello. Where have you come from?" Leo asked, giving her a friendly rub on her belly.

"Wha—?" Tomasz mumbled, half rising and squinting sleepily.

"We've got a visitor."

"Oh, hello, girl," Tomasz said. He yawned and began scratching the dog's ears. "You're a beauty, aren't you? Yes, you are. Look at your lovely brown eyes."

The dog wagged her tail, jumped up, and put her front paws on Tomasz's shoulders. She licked his face and then jumped up to do the same to Leo.

"Get off, you daft thing!" he laughed, pushing her away so she rolled over and lay on her back again. He rubbed the ribs that poked from beneath her black-and-white fur.

"She's a bit thin. She must be hungry."

"She's not the only one," Tomasz said, peering blearily through the half-open door. "Let's see if we can find something to eat."

They left the woodshed and crept over to the house to make sure it was empty. There was no sign of anyone, so they felt safe to explore the huge garden. At the far end was a small pond, and the white ducks sitting around the edge quickly flapped away into the water as the dog went bounding toward them. Leo and Tomasz searched in the hedges bordering the garden and found three duck eggs.

"Perfect," Leo said. "One each, and one for the dog."

He cracked open an egg and laid it on the ground for the dog to lap up, and then he and Tomasz used the tip of the knife to make small holes in either end of their eggs so they could suck out the raw liquid.

"Well, we're going to have to leave you now," Leo said, bending down and giving the dog a final tickle behind the ears. But when they started along the track, the dog followed them.

"Shoo! Go on home!" Tomasz shouted and stamped his feet. The dog ran back a few paces and then stopped and sat down, cocking her head to one side and wagging her tail—as if she was enjoying this new game. As soon as they started walking again, she got to her feet and ran after them, dashing past them and then stopping in the middle of the track to wait for them to catch up.

"Home!" Leo said, throwing a stone in the direction they'd come from. The dog bounded after the stone, picked it up in her mouth, and then hurried back to lay it at Leo's feet.

"Pay no attention to her. She'll soon get tired of us," Tomasz said. But half an hour later, there she was, still trotting about forty meters behind them.

"Go…home!" Leo ordered.

The dog sat and wagged her tail, as if waiting for another stone. Tomasz picked up a stick and ran toward her, waving it threateningly, but she just barked and jumped up, trying to catch hold of it.

"What are we going to do, Leo? We can't just let her come with us, can we?"

"Perhaps she's a stray. She's thin, and she doesn't seem to have a home to go to…"

"We can't keep her. How are we going to feed her? We haven't got food for ourselves," Tomasz said, and then he laughed as the dog grabbed his stick and started pulling at it. "I've got an idea. We don't encourage her, don't look back or anything and if she's still with us when…" He looked around and pointed. "…When we get to that ridge, we'll let her stay."

The ridge was over a kilometer away, but when they finally got to the top of it and turned around, the dog was still following them. She stopped and looked at them. They sat down, and Leo called, "Come on, then—come here."

She hesitated, but when he slapped his hand against his thigh and called again, she came bounding up and almost knocked them over, leaping up, licking their faces, running around, and barking.

"What are we going to call her?" Leo said.

"Nuisance," Tomasz replied with a laugh.

"No. She's beautiful."

"What about 'Bella'? It's Italian for beautiful. My father—the cobbler—always used to say the very word sounded like a beautiful woman."

"Bella…Bella," Leo said, trying it out—but it didn't seem quite right for a dog. "What about Bel?" At that moment the dog looked up and barked.

"She likes it," Tomasz said. "Bel, it is."

The sun was hot, so they moved into the shade of a tree at the edge of the ridge and sat, looking down at the River Wisła. The brownish gray water was running slower than before, swirling in large, lazy eddies. A barge came chugging upstream, its smoke rising almost vertically in the still air. Two skiffs floated downstream, about ten meters apart, with a man in each of them. They were dragging a rope between them, and when they hauled it up, fish flashed silver in the bulging net, and shouts of success echoed across the water and up to the ridge.

"Hey, what's this?" Leo asked, as a strange craft begin to swing around a bend in the river and snaked its way down toward them.

As it drew closer, they saw that it was a long, long raft of tree trunks. Each section of the raft was made up of twenty-four logs, twelve wide and two deep, which were nailed together with planks and joined to the other sections by ropes and chains.

There were fifteen sections in all, with a man standing on every third one using long poles to steer and keep the raft in a straight line. On the middle section there was a little hut with a couple of men sitting outside it on chairs. The men looked up and waved, and Leo and Tomasz waved back.

"That's the way to travel," Tomasz said. "They're probably taking those logs all the way down to Danzig."

"That would be good," Leo agreed.

The raft had been making smooth progress past them, but now there was a loud cry from the man standing on the first section. He ran to the front of the logs and thrust his pole into the water, and then suddenly went flying backward as his pole shot out of his hands and the whole front section jolted. It had hit a sand bank just under the water.

The raft came to a juddering halt, and all the sections banged into each other, sending the men reeling with the impact. A couple of them fell down, and one tumbled overboard into the water. He quickly clambered back up again and then joined the others who were rushing toward the front of the raft. They began pushing with their poles, easing the raft off the sand bank and then moving it sideways toward open water. As the raft floated free, it was swept forward on the current again. Ten minutes later it had disappeared around a bend downstream.

Leo stretched and stood up. Bel had paid no attention to all the excitement on the raft and was curled up, asleep, but as soon as she heard the boys move, she jumped up, tail wagging and ready to go.

They walked all afternoon and then stopped at a small clump of trees that would keep the dew off them for the night. They hunted around and found some wild mushrooms to eat, but when they offered one to Bel, she merely sniffed at it and walked away.

Leo had noticed a couple of rabbit runs just before the clump of trees, so he went back to look at them.

"Pity we haven't got any twine," he said. "A lot of rabbits come through here. I could have made a snare."

"I've got some thread," Tomasz said, rummaging in his sack. "I snaffled it just before we left old Plinski's."

Leo tied the thread to a thick bramble overhanging one of the runs and made a noose with a running knot that he arranged in the foliage about twelve centimeters above the ground. They went back to the clump of trees, and while Leo started digging a pit, Tomasz set out for a cottage they could see in the distance to cadge some fire.

Leo had just completed the pit and filled it with dry moss and kindling, when Tomasz came back carrying a piece of glowing charcoal on a flat stone.

"It was an old woman living on her own, and she didn't want

to open the door at first. But when she saw my sweet face at the window, she couldn't resist," Tomasz said with a grin.

He placed the charcoal on the moss, and soon the little fire was burning brightly. Bel curled up beside it and put her head on her paws to watch the dancing flames.

"Well, even if we don't catch anything, it'll be good to have a fire for the night," Leo said.

But just as the last glow of day was fading, they went back to check the snare, and there was a large rabbit. The bramble was bent and pulled out of place, so it was obvious that the rabbit had put up a struggle, but it had simply drawn the noose tighter and tighter until it had strangled itself. Leo used Tomasz's knife to gut the rabbit. He fed the heart and lungs and liver to Bel, and then he cut off the head and feet and skinned it. They spitted the carcass on a long stick and sat on either side of the fire, turning it slowly until it was cooked.

It was good to lie down with a full belly, with the comforting flicker of the fire nearby and the warmth of Bel curled up between them. Above, the stars peeped down, coming and going amid the leaves of the trees, as the earth slowly revolved through the velvety night toward dawn.

Chapter 26

THEY MADE SLOW PROGRESS DOWN THE WISŁA BECAUSE FINDING food took up so much time—they would set snares for rabbits or try to catch fish by staking a stream and spearing them. Sometimes they were lucky, but when they failed to catch anything, they had to resort to stealing eggs and vegetables from farms. Even that took time, as they had to wait and watch to make sure there was no one around. Once, they were nearly caught when a farmer came back suddenly and chased them across the fields. Leo hated stealing from farms because he knew how his own family struggled to make a living from the soil, but he couldn't ignore the growling hunger in his belly.

One day on the outskirts of a town, they saw two Jews walking ahead of them down the dirt road. They were wearing black hats and long black coats, and they had prayer shawls across their shoulders. Usually Leo and Tomasz avoided going through towns, not wanting to meet policemen, but when Leo turned off the road to head across the fields, Tomasz hesitated.

"Oh, come on, let's just take the road," he said. "It'll save hours."

It was a hot morning, and Leo didn't need much persuading. It was only when they reached the center of the town that he realized the real reason why they had come this way. The Jews turned left down a side road, and Tomasz stopped and watched as they went into a synagogue.

"Leo…" he said.

"What?"

"Can you wait for me?" Tomasz said. He looked at Leo, and there was a shy, almost embarrassed smile on his lips. "I want to go in. I want to see what Jews do. After all, I'm one of them."

Leo shrugged. "Yes, if you want. I'll wait for you in the shade over there."

He sat down with Bel on the grassy bank opposite the synagogue and watched as Tomasz went up to the door. A very tall Jew with a gray beard and a fur hat was standing on the steps, and he bent down to listen as Tomasz spoke to him. There was a long conversation, and then the man went inside. Tomasz turned around to Leo and spread his arms wide in a gesture of uncertainty. A short while later, the man came out again and said something to him. Tomasz nodded and then the man placed a black skullcap on his head, gently took his hand, and led him inside the building.

Leo waited. Bel wandered along the bank, sniffing the grass and the trees before coming back and sitting at Leo's feet. He stroked her and listened to the faint sound of chanting that drifted across the road. A farmer walked past, driving two cows in front of him, and Leo noticed how the man glanced across at the synagogue and crossed himself. Bel got up and ran after the cows, barking, and then she lost interest and trotted across to the synagogue and sat at the base of the steps, looking up at the door as if she was hoping Tomasz would come out.

Leo went over to join Bel, and he sat on the bottom step. He could hear the chanting more clearly now, and he closed his eyes to try and make out some of the words but he couldn't. The chanting was like nothing he'd ever heard before, though, and he found himself swaying backward and forward, lost in the sound, until Bel growled. He opened his eyes and looked up to find a burly man standing in front of him. He was wearing a dirty smock, and he was swaying, as if he had drunk too much.

"You stinking little Jewboy," he said, his lips curling in hatred.

Leo was too astonished to speak. The man raised his fist and moved toward him menacingly, but he stopped when Bel snarled and got to her feet. The man aimed a kick at her, but she skipped out of range and he staggered sideways. He steadied himself and stumbled away, but after a couple of paces, he turned back and spat at Leo. The thick spittle landed on Leo's waistcoat, and when the man had gone he went over to the road and wiped it on the grass.

A shiver of disgust shook him as he looked at the wet patch on the waistcoat. It was obvious that the man was drunk, but Leo had never been treated like that before. He knew that people didn't like Jews. Back in his village, the Catholics and Protestants didn't really get along with each other, but the one thing they agreed on was that Jews were nothing but trouble—Jews and gypsies. Gypsies would steal the clothes off your back, everyone said, and Jews would bleed you dry if you got into debt with them. He'd even heard one peasant blame the Jews when his cow had given birth to a dead calf. And Leo realized that, somehow, he had absorbed all this and thought it was true, until now.

What was a Jew? That man had hated him and spat at him because he thought he was a Jew. Tomasz was a Jew, but he hadn't even known he was until last year. It didn't make any sense. Would Tomasz bleed him dry? Of course not. He shared everything. They had only known each other a short time, but already Leo felt that Tomasz was like a brother to him.

He was still busy thinking about all this when people began coming out of the synagogue. They stood around, smiling and talking to each other for a while, and then they shook hands and went their separate ways. It reminded Leo of exactly what he and his family did after church.

Tomasz was the last to come out, and Bel immediately got up, wanting to greet him but Leo held her back. Tomasz stood on the steps, talking to the man with the gray beard and fur hat, and Leo noticed how thin and bony his friend was. With his big ears and the eager expression on his face, he looked like a little boy next to the tall man—like Jozef when he looked up at Papa.

The conversation went on for a long time and when it finally came to an end, the man shook Tomasz's hand. Then, he solemnly bent down and kissed the top of his head. A huge smile lit up Tomasz's face, and he was still smiling as he walked across the road to Leo. Yet his eyes glistened with tears.

"His brother is a rabbi in New York," he said, nodding toward the man who was going back into the synagogue. "He's given me his address, and he told me that he'll look after us when we get to America."

And suddenly, the tears overflowed and ran down Tomasz's cheeks. He sat down on the grassy bank, put his head down on his knees, and shook with sobs.

"What is it? What's wrong?" Leo asked, putting his arm around his friend's shoulders and letting him cry until he stopped.

Tomasz raised his head and gave a little half laugh. "I'm crying because I'm happy," he said, sniffing and wiping the tears from his face. "He was so nice to me. And all the time I was in there…I couldn't understand a word…It was all in Hebrew, but…I felt as if I knew what it meant. And it made me feel…good."

Leo remembered the way he'd been affected by the chanting, and he nodded.

"When we get to America, I'm going to be a Jew. A proper Jew," Tomasz said. "But we'll still be friends, won't we?"

Leo looked into Tomasz's worried eyes and laughed. "Of course we will!" He was almost on the point of saying something about the man who'd spat at him, but he didn't.

They walked through the center of the town and were just passing the town hall when a bell began ringing from its rooftop. A moment later, another bell joined in from a church across the square. Then another, more distant, and another, until the air was filled with the clanging.

"What's happening?" Leo called as a man burst out of the town hall and ran to a horse tied up against the wall.

"It's war," the man cried as he put papers into his saddlebag. "France has declared war. Our army is massing on the border, and a general mobilization has been announced. All men of military age will have to join the army. It's war. God save King Wilhelm. Victory will be ours."

He untied his horse, jumped into the saddle, and galloped away down the road, waving his hat and shouting the news.

Within minutes, the streets were filled with people, and in the rising hubbub, one word could be heard again and again: "War! War!"

Chapter 27

FEAR AND UNCERTAINTY GRIPPED THE COUNTRYSIDE.
When Leo and Tomasz walked past, peasants looked up from their work in the fields and watched them suspiciously. Once, when they stopped to chat with some young children playing outside a house, their mother came running out the door and anxiously called the children inside. Wherever they went, people were talking about war and cholera.

In one village, a man was standing on the steps of a church. He had ripped open his ragged shirt and was beating his breast wildly in front of a small group of women, who were looking up at him in awe.

"The prophecies are being fulfilled," he shouted. "It is written that there will be war. War and pestilence. Behold the wrath of God."

He staggered down the steps, and the women moved back. He picked up a handful of dust, showered it over his head, and rubbed it in so it streaked his sweaty face and matted his hair.

"We are all sinners! We must repent!" he howled, and the women moaned and crossed themselves. "Satan is roaming the world, stealing souls, and only Mother Church stands against him. But soon our Lord will return. The Second Coming is at hand!"

Bel ran toward the man and stopped in front of him, barking. Without a single pause in his tirade about Satan and sin, the man picked up a stone and hurled it at Bel. It hit her directly in the ribs, and she yelped in pain and skittered away down the street. Leo and

Tomasz gave chase, but the faster they ran, the faster Bel ran, and by the time they got to the edge of the village, they were out of breath and had to stop. They watched as Bel kept going and finally disappeared down the dusty road.

They came across her about twenty minutes later lying by the side of the road, licking her wound. She growled when they bent down and tried to see the damage.

"Shhh, girl," Leo said, gently laying his hand on her head, even though she was baring her fangs. "Shhh, Bel. It's all right."

He stroked her head, and her lips settled back over her teeth. Her tail wagged once, but when he reached out to touch her side, there was another low growl in her throat.

They stood up and walked a few steps down the road. Then, they stopped and called her. She painfully rose to her feet and limped toward them.

"Good girl," Leo said. She wagged her tail, and then, panting and treading gingerly, began to follow them. Her fur was stained with blood, but within an hour, she seemed to have walked the pain away. She quickly took up her usual position, running ahead of them and looking back from time to time to make sure they were still coming.

It was Bel who found the pond. They saw her disappear off the track and then heard her yapping excitedly, so they followed the noise along a narrow path through the tall ferns. Just beyond a line of poplar trees, they came upon the large pond. It was perfectly round and the reflection of the sky made the water look blue but, when they peered down, it was crystal clear and they could see every detail of the sand and gravel on the bottom.

The day was so hot, and the water so inviting, that Leo immediately stripped off his clothes and waded out into the middle of the pond. The water was chilly at first, but when he ducked his head under, it felt perfect, and he lay on his back and floated. Bel paddled out and swam around and around him, obviously enjoying it as much as he was.

"Come on!" he called to Tomasz, who was still waiting at the edge.

"Can you stand?" Tomasz asked.

"Yes, look. It only comes up to my chest. It's great."

Tomasz took off his waistcoat and shirt and then undid his belt and lowered his trousers. He took a couple of paces into the water and then stumbled and stopped as it suddenly came up to his waist. He laughed nervously and splashed water in Leo's direction.

"Does it get deeper?" he asked.

"Not much. I showed you."

"But there might be holes."

"There aren't. Can't you swim?" Leo asked.

"Of course I can."

Moving carefully and peering intently at his feet in the clear water, Tomasz made his way slowly to the middle. Leo could see the goose bumps on his skin.

"You have to duck under, Tom."

Tomasz smiled and slowly lowered himself until the water covered his shoulders.

"It's good, isn't it?" Tomasz said, but he didn't sound sure.

There was a splash, and Bel swam past them, heading for the shore. She stepped out of the water and immediately shook herself, sending spray all over their clothes.

"Bel! Oh no," Leo shouted as Bel settled herself down on the pile of clothes. "Get off."

But Bel didn't move, so he made his way to the side and jumped ashore.

"Get off, you stupid dog." He laughed, pulling her off the clothes. "Look what she's done. They're soaking."

He lifted the damp shirts and laid them out in the sun. Then, he grabbed Tomasz's belt, which was lying across his trousers. The belt was heavy—very heavy—and one end swung and cracked against his shin.

"What have you got in this belt? It weighs a—" He stopped when he saw Tomasz spin around with an expression of alarm.

Tomasz began striding toward the shore, his hands beating the water to help him move quickly. But before he reached the land, Leo felt along the belt and knew.

"So that's where you keep it," Leo said, holding out the belt to the dripping Tomasz. "I thought you were making it up."

"Making what up?" Tomasz said, snatching the belt.

"The silver coins," Leo said. Then, after a moment, he added, "The man you killed."

Tomasz was silent while they both got dressed. Then he sat down and stared at the water. Leo sat next to him.

"I thought it was one of your stories," Leo said apologetically. "You know—you tell stories."

"You're my friend," Tomasz said quietly. "I told you because you're my friend. Why would I lie about killing someone?"

"I…I just didn't believe you had money. We've almost starved and—"

"I told you," Tomasz cut in. "It's for us—for America, for our future. You don't understand. I was lost and on my own. I couldn't go home, and I knew I had to go away. But I was scared about going all that way alone. Then I met you, and when you told me you were going to America too, I suddenly realized the truth. We didn't meet by chance. God brought us together, because we're going to be great men together. Don't laugh. We are. I feel it. Listen, the money in this belt is what's going to make the difference. Thousands of people spend all their savings to get to America, and they arrive there with nothing. Not us. We'll walk, we'll sleep rough, we'll work, we'll go without food. It might be hard, but we'll get there, and when we do, we'll have this money. That's why we'll succeed. Don't you see?"

It was impossible to resist Tomasz's enthusiasm, and he was right. It would be a waste to spend money on food when they could catch rabbits or fish. It would be a waste to spend it on train fares when they could walk—all the way to the sea, if necessary. Leo felt filled with energy and hope. He took the belt out of Tomasz's hands.

"Here's to our future!" he said, holding the belt up and feeling the weight of it. "When did you put the coins in here?"

"I bought the leather when I was in Posen and sewed them in. It was the safest place I could think of."

"It's so heavy. No wonder you walk slowly," Leo joked, handing the belt back. "I ought to give you a piggyback ride."

"That's a good idea," Tomasz said, and sprang up onto Leo's back.

Leo's knees buckled and they fell to the ground. They rolled around laughing while Bel barked and jumped on them.

Chapter 28

THE HOT WEATHER BROKE WITH A SPECTACULAR STORM.
Leo and Tomasz watched the jags of lightning from a small shepherd's shelter that shuddered when the thunder roared and cracked around them. Bel cowered between their legs, her eyes white with fright at every flash and boom. The rain beat down, obscuring the distant trees, until nearly nightfall. When it eased off, they set out across the soggy fields, hoping to find somewhere better to spend the night.

They had just seen the lights of a small village in the distance when the rain, driven by a fierce wind, began to thrash down again. They ducked into a barn and stood in the doorway waiting for the downpour to stop, but it was soon obvious that it had set in for the night. There were no lights or sign of life from the house on the other side of the yard, so they lay down in some straw at the back of the barn and fell asleep to the sound of the howling wind and the splattering rain.

Sometime during the night, Leo woke to the sound of whimpering. He thought it was Bel but then he realized it was coming from Tomasz, who was in the grip of another one of his bad dreams. Leo shook his shoulder gently. Tomasz stirred briefly and then settled back into sleep, the nightmare banished.

The rain pelted down the whole of the next day. The puddles grew larger and larger, and water started to pour off the fields until a raging stream was coursing across the yard and down onto the road. Water lapped into the entrance of the barn, and little rivulets burst through gaps in the wooden walls, soaking the straw.

Leo and Tomasz climbed a ladder up to a narrow storage platform and sat there, staring at the rain falling onto the flooded yard. From up there, they could see that the farmhouse had been abandoned. The roof had caved in at the top, and the windows were broken. At least they knew no one was going to drive them out into the rain.

Although they were dry, they grew hungrier and hungrier, and the damp chill began to seep into their bones. Leo went down the ladder and searched through the straw hoping to find something to eat, but there was nothing. They spent the rest of the day staring mournfully at the deluge. Then, as the light faded, they covered themselves and Bel with old sacks and shivered their way through the night, slipping in and out of sleep.

Toward dawn, the rain finally stopped, and they walked out into a waterlogged world. Everything dripped, and the air was filled with the sound of water rushing in ditches and streams.

They walked to the village and found people emerging from their houses to look at their flooded gardens and yards. They went into a shop and spent the last of the money they'd earned at Plinski's on some bread and a salami. Then, when they reached the outskirts of the village, Tomasz produced some carrots he'd snaffled while Leo had been paying the shopkeeper. They sat on a fallen log by the side of the road, cut off a chunk of salami for Bel, and then set about filling their own hungry stomachs while she sat at their feet, hoping for more.

When they finished eating, they climbed the hill to the top of a ridge and looked down toward the Wisła. The rain had turned the river into a churning, brown torrent that had broken its banks and flooded the fields. A barge was trying to battle its way upstream, but despite the throbbing of its engine, it seemed almost stationary as the waters raged around it and splashed up over its prow. They watched its slow progress as it beat against the current and finally rounded the bend.

Downstream, they could just make out the distant church towers and tall buildings of Graudenz, perched on the slope above the Wisła.

Tomasz pointed toward the smoke rising from factory chimneys. "Perhaps we can find some work there for a couple of days."

They set off along the ridge.

For a while, they walked along the edge of a steep cliff where the river foamed and churned directly at its base. Then the slope grew gentler, and there was a strip of flat land below them. Through the trees on the slope, they glimpsed a log raft like the one they'd seen before, but this one had only four sections. The front three sections were tied to stakes on the bank, but the last section had broken loose and a man was struggling to stop it from being swept out into the middle of the river. He was hanging on to the rope and digging his feet in to brace himself against the surge of the water. They could see that if he didn't get that section under control, the power of the river would sweep it outward, and the other three sections would be pulled from their moorings. They scrambled down the slope and ran across to help him.

"Grab the rope and hold on," he shouted above the noise of the roaring water. "I've got to drive the stake back in."

Leo and Tomasz took the rope and, as the man let go, they were jerked forward by the power of the water tugging at the logs. The raft swung farther away from the bank, and they were dragged, slipping and sliding, across the wet ground toward the river's edge. The man grabbed hold of the rope again, and the three of them managed to haul the fourth section of the raft back toward the bank.

"Wrap the rope around your hands and dig your heels in," the man yelled. "That's right. Now brace yourselves and just hold it steady there. Can you do that?"

They nodded and, slowly, the man lifted his hands away from the rope. Once again they felt the full force of the river as they took the strain. The rope bit into their hands and almost jerked their arms from their sockets, but they were ready this time, and, leaning back, they held fast. Behind them, they could hear the man hammering the stake into position.

The rope was crushing Leo's hands, and he could feel his bones crunching against each other. When Tomasz's feet began to slip on the wet grass and they started to slide forward again, Leo felt as if he couldn't take the pain anymore. He was just about to let go when the man rushed to their side and began hauling them back toward the stake.

"That's it," he called. "Hold tight while I loop this over. That's it. You can let go."

The rope tightened around the stake, and the man made a couple of extra loops ending with a clove hitch. He picked up a sledgehammer and pounded the wood farther into the ground before running off to check the moorings of the other sections of the raft. Leo and Tomasz were comparing the rope marks on their hands when he came back.

"Show me," he said, and he examined their hands, gently pressing and prodding. "You'll be fine. Nothing's broken, but it must have hurt like damnation. I owe you my thanks. I'd have lost the whole raft without you. The least I can do is offer you some breakfast. I was just about to cook it when that damned float broke loose."

The man had made himself a little camp on the slope. He had strung a rope between two trees and staked out a canvas sheet over it to make a kind of tent. There was a fire burning brightly in a pail and a frying pan standing next to it. He slung three large pieces of meat in the pan and placed it on the top of the pail. Soon there was the mouthwatering smell of sizzling meat.

"Your dog?" he asked, pointing to Bel, who was standing some way off, unsure if the man would welcome her or not. "Come on then. Here's a bit for you."

He threw the raw meat toward Bel, and she tiptoed forward and wolfed it down. The man settled back onto his haunches and occasionally turned the meat in the pan until it was ready. Then he put the pieces on a big metal plate. "Right. I haven't got enough knives and forks, so you'll have to use your hands. By the way, you can't eat with a man without knowing his name. I'm Patryk."

They introduced themselves and began eating. It was good to have hot food, and they wolfed it down almost as quickly as Bel.

"Was that pork?" Tomasz asked, licking his fingers.

"Certainly was," Patryk said.

"Delicious. I shouldn't eat it, though," Tomasz said.

"Oh? Why not?" Patryk asked.

"Because I'm going to be a Jew when I get to America."

Patryk laughed and slapped his knee. "When you get to America, eh? Well, then, you can worry about pork when the time comes! How're you planning to get there?"

"Catch a boat in Danzig," Leo replied.

"That's where I'm taking these logs. I've been floating timber down there since I wasn't much older than you two. There's always a big demand for good Galician pine in Danzig."

"We saw a raft much bigger than yours. It had fifteen sections," Tomasz said.

"They're called floats, not sections. Yes, I've done those big ones too, but by the time you pay all the raft riders, you make less money than with a smaller raft like this."

"You handle it all on your own?" Leo asked.

"It's just about possible, but it's hellish work. I had a man to help on this trip but he walked out on me in Thorn because he was worried about getting caught up in this damn war." Patryk looked away at the raft and then back at them. "I could do with a couple of hands, and floating to Danzig would be quicker than walking. It's hard work, mind you."

"On that thing?" Tomasz asked, looking anxiously at the raft rocking on the surging waters. "Bit rough, isn't it?"

"Oh, it'll be as smooth as a baby's bottom come tomorrow. What d'you say?"

"Yes!" Leo immediately said, but then he saw the look of fear on Tomasz's face. "I mean, we'll talk about it."

"Go ahead and talk," Patryk said. "I'll wash up." He picked up the plate and the pan and wandered down to the river.

"Don't you want to, Tom?"

"Of course I want to. Like he says, it's quicker, isn't it?"

"Honest? I don't mind walking," Leo said.

"No, it makes sense," Tomasz said. "We'll go with him."

Chapter 29

IT ACTUALLY TOOK FIVE DAYS BEFORE THE WISŁA CALMED DOWN, but it was good to rest and eat properly. Patryk was a good shot and he killed some ducks and a couple of rabbits, so there was plenty to eat. He took a liking to Bel and always threw her a lump of meat before the meal, so she began following him around in the hope that there would be more.

In the relaxed times after they had eaten, they chatted about their lives. Tomasz and Leo told Patryk about their childhoods, and he told them about his life on the river. He was a good storyteller, and they loved listening to his tales of adventures and accidents on the rapids in the gorges upstream.

"Don't look so worried, Tomasz. From here on down to Danzig, it's plain sailing," Patryk said reassuringly, and added, "As long as you don't get stuck on a sand bank, of course."

Then he burst out laughing as Tomasz's face fell again.

They cast off early on the sixth day.

It was a beautiful morning, and the river was running much slower. Patryk stood on the first float. Leo was on the third with Bel by his side, and Tomasz was on the fourth. At Patryk's signal, they used their long poles to push away from the bank, and the current began to carry them out toward the center of the stream. At that very moment, the sun began to stream over the ridge and a kingfisher flashed past them across the water.

Leo's heart filled with excitement. They were gliding smoothly downstream, and within a week, so Patryk had said, they would be in Danzig. Suddenly their dream seemed within grasp.

"It's great, isn't it?" he called, turning and smiling at Tomasz, who was standing rather unsteadily at the rear of the raft. Tomasz nodded.

"Can we move about?" Leo called to Patryk.

"Of course you can."

"What about the pole?" Leo asked

"It's called a pike," Patryk said. "Just leave it in the center of the float so it doesn't roll off. And be ready to get back to your post if I tell you to."

Leo laid down his pike and made his way along the logs to the back of his float. The movement of the raft made it difficult to walk, but he found it was easier if he kept his feet wide apart to steady himself. He reached the end of his float and looked down at the water between him and the fourth float. It was only a narrow gap and Bel skipped over it easily, but Leo still took a deep breath before he jumped across. He landed on the other side and slipped slightly on the damp logs, but he managed not to fall. He made his way down to where Tomasz was standing, still holding his pike tightly in his hand. He looked nervous.

"It's easier if you stand with your feet apart," Leo said. "And Patryk said we could put the pikes down."

Gingerly, Tomasz laid his pike down and then stood with his arms slightly held out to the side for balance.

"It's the first time I've been on a boat," he said.

"Me too," Leo said. "Let's move around a bit to get used to it."

They walked up and down the float a couple of times, and Tomasz became more and more confident, although he hesitated a long time before he followed Leo over the gap and onto the next float. But when he finally jumped and landed safely, he laughed out loud and threw his arms in the air in triumph. They sat down in the middle of the float and looked up at the city walls of Graudenz, high on the ridge.

Patryk gave them a running commentary on the sites they were passing. "That's the nunnery—won't get much fun with the ladies there!...That's the tower of St. Nicholas Church...Those big buildings are the granaries, and the chimneys you can just see behind are the brickworks...Look at this barge coming toward us. It's probably going into the docks over there. Hold tight. We're going to catch its wash in a minute."

The wash from the barge rolled toward them in a series of waves, rocking the raft and splashing over the sides of the logs. Tomasz let out a little whoop of excitement—"Wahhhay!"—and stood up with a big grin on his face, only to fall back down as the barge suddenly tipped again.

Patryk had warned them it would be hard work, and it was. For much of the time, the raft floated gently down the center of the Wisła, but when it veered off course or the river curved or there was other traffic ahead, Patryk yelled commands and they had to run backward and forward, using the pikes as rudders to help steer. The pikes were heavy and long, and dragging them through the water made their arm muscles ache with the strain.

From the very first, Bel was completely at home on the raft, racing along the tree trunks and barking with excitement, but Leo and Tomasz took longer to get used to it. Patryk told them that they'd find it easier to walk and work if they were barefoot, so they took his advice and left their boots stowed securely in the "dry box" he had constructed on the second float. By the time they docked for the night at Neuenburg, they had become so accustomed to the raft's movement that their legs felt wobbly and strange when they jumped ashore to secure the raft.

Patryk left them a phosphorus match and told them to collect firewood and light the fire while he set off up the steep path to the town to buy food for the evening meal. Once the fire was burning in the pail, they could sit down and rest at last.

"Oh, I ache everywhere," Tomasz groaned, stretching out.

"Me too. And the blisters on my hands," Leo added. "Still, think about how far we've come. It would have taken days of walking."

"It's good to be back on land, though. The river's a bit too watery for me," Tomasz said.

He thought for a moment about what he'd just said, and then he snorted with laughter.

"Too watery! You idiot," Leo said, punching Tomasz's arm. Then a chuckle rose up, and he was too tired and weak to resist it. He fell backward and collapsed into helpless giggles. Tomasz joined in.

They lay on their backs for a while, looking up at the town of Neuenburg perched on the ridge high above them. The setting sun was striking the crumbling ancient walls and glowing richly on the thousands of red tiles of the steep church roof.

"Tom, it's going to happen," Leo said, turning and looking at his friend. "We're going to America."

"I know. A week, perhaps two, and we'll be on that boat bound across the ocean."

A golden light was bathing the buildings of the town. Swallows, martins, and swifts were swooping across the orange and blue sky, hunting for insects. A few wispy clouds were turning from white to pink to gray as the night approached, and Leo was filled with more hope and contentment than he had ever known.

Patryk brought back some fish and potatoes, and he cut them

up and tossed them in a pan over the fire. By the time they had stretched a rope between a couple of trees and draped the canvas sheet across it, pegging the sides out to make a tent for the night, the food was cooked. Patryk had his fork and Tomasz quickly sharpened a couple of twigs for himself and Leo, and they ate the crisp pieces of fish and potatoes directly out of the pan.

When they finished eating, Leo and Tomasz felt exhausted and drowsy.

"You're not coming into town, then?" Patryk asked, seeing them both yawn.

"What for?" Tomasz mumbled, looking longingly at the blanket inside the tent.

"Raft rider's reward—wine, women, and song!" Patryk said, dousing the fire in the pail.

They shook their heads and, as soon as he started up the hill toward the town, they crawled under the canvas and lay down. Bel took her usual place, snuggled between them, and they fell asleep.

The sun was already high in the sky when they finally awoke the next morning, but there was no sign of Patryk. They sat on the riverbank and watched some men fishing, but when the church bell struck noon from high above them, they decided to go in search of him. They walked up the path and onto the cobbled lane that led through the gateway into the old town. Just as they passed through the brick archway and came out into the bright sunshine, they saw Patryk step out of one of the houses along the street.

He turned back and kissed a young woman who was leaning out of the doorway. Then, with a big smile on his lips, he headed toward them. There was a spring in his step, and Leo realized that, with his tanned face, curly black hair, broad shoulders, and jaunty air, he was a handsome man.

"Sorry I'm a bit late," he called breezily, and then he jerked his thumb back to the house he'd left. "I got caught up."

"Is she someone you know?" Tomasz asked.

"Well, let's just say, I do now!" Patryk laughed. "Anyway, let's get out of town before her husband gets back."

Chapter 30

THE RIVER CURRENT GREW VERY SLUGGISH, AND THEY DRIFTED along so slowly that there was barely a breeze as they moved. The sun beat down, and Bel lay near the edge of the raft, panting. After a while, she stood up and leaned over the side to lap at the water, but she overbalanced and fell in. Leo had to rush across the float to pull her out.

Patryk rammed two pikes between the logs, slung a rope between them, and hung a canvas sheet over the rope to provide a bit of shade. He lay down and fell asleep, leaving Leo and Tomasz in charge. The river was wide, and there was very little traffic, so they didn't have much to do. But they felt rather nervous as they stood at the front of the raft, pikes at the ready, staring at the water ahead for shallows or rocks.

"I suppose I'll have to get circumcised when I'm a Jew," Tomasz said.

"What made you think of that?" Leo asked.

"Just thinking. They do that, though, don't they—the Jews? I wonder if it hurts?" He shivered at the thought.

"I thought they only did it to babies."

"That's true," Tomasz said, brightening up. "I'll be fifteen by the time we get to America. They wouldn't make a fifteen-year-old drop his trousers and cut bits off him, would they? Well, if they try, I'll just tell them I'll do all the other stuff to be a Jew, but I won't do that."

The sunlight shimmered on the river, and the silver flashes almost blinded them as they peered intently at the water for any sign of danger—a telltale wave rising up over a rock, or a whirling disturbance over a sandbank. A barge, piled high with coal, chugged upstream, sending its wake toward them. They braced themselves and stood steady when the raft bucked and rocked as the waves passed underneath.

As the sun began to dip low in the sky, Patryk woke up and came to stand next to them at the front of the raft.

"Hey, that's Eichwald," he said, pointing to a small collection of houses across the fields. "Is that all we've done—Neuenburg to Eichwald? I was hoping to get to Mewe tonight."

"We can't go faster than the river!" Leo said, hurt that Patryk wasn't pleased with the way they'd controlled the raft.

"No, of course you can't, lad," Patryk said, ruffling Leo's hair by way of apology. "You've done really well. It's just that there's a certain young lady I was hoping to see in Mewe tonight!"

"Have you got women in every town?" Tomasz said, and Leo heard the tone of disapproval in his voice.

"No, only in about half of them!" Patryk joked. "Why, are you jealous?"

"No," Tomasz said coldly.

But Patryk didn't seem to notice, and he pointed to a group of willows growing on the riverbank ahead. "We'll put in over there for the night—shoot a rabbit or two for the evening meal, and get some shut-eye and be ready for an early start tomorrow. Hard down to port!"

Tomasz and Leo dug their pikes into the water, and the raft changed direction and slowly headed for the shore.

"Well done, lads. That was nigh on perfect!" Patryk said as he slung a rope around one of the willows and the raft came to a standstill.

174

Patryk left Leo and Tomasz in charge of setting up camp, and he went off hunting. He was gone a long time, but he came back carrying a couple of rabbits he'd already skinned and gutted, so they were able to put them straight onto spits and hang them over the fire.

It was dark by the time they'd finished eating. The night was warm, and Leo and Tomasz weren't sleepy, so they lay next to the fire staring up at the star-filled night while Patryk talked.

"I met a farmer while I was hunting. He said that there are all kinds of rumors flying around about this war. Some reckon the French have invaded Prussia, and others say Prussia has invaded France, but no one's sure if fighting has really started yet. Apparently, the Prussian army is already over three hundred thousand strong. They're calling up everyone of military age."

"Not you," Leo said.

"I'm not Prussian, am I? I was born in the Kingdom of Poland, although they call it Vistulaland now—stupid name. It's just part of the Russian Empire! They might as well call us Russian and be done with it!"

"I don't understand it," Tomasz said.

"Nobody understands it, lad. We tell ourselves we're Polish, but our poor country doesn't exist. It's been gobbled up and spat out in three pieces that belong to Prussia, Russia, and Austria, and they can do what they like with us. They're even trying to outlaw Polish as a language now. The whole world is crazy, and it's getting crazier. Do you know what I heard the other day? The Pope has declared that he is infallible."

"What does that mean?"

"It means that he can't be wrong. If he says black is white, we have to believe him. If he says Bel is a saint in doggy disguise, we have to believe him. It's mad."

"But he's the Pope! He's God's emissary," Leo protested, remembering the things he'd heard the priest say in church.

"He's a man, Leo, an ordinary man. He's got the same body as you and me, and the same mind as you and me. He's just managed to scramble his way to the top of the heap in the church. That takes some doing, I grant you. But it doesn't mean that he's closer to God. It just means he's rougher and tougher than the rest of them."

Leo's face burned with shock and confusion. He'd never heard anyone say bad things about the Pope before. The Pope was the Papa, the shepherd who looked after his flock. He was a kind man who loved all his Catholic children and kept them on the road to heaven.

He crossed himself, and Patryk laughed. "Ah, you're a good child of the church, Leo. They've stopped you from thinking for yourself. What about you, Tomasz? Are you in their grip too?"

"I'm going to be a Jew, aren't I?"

"That's right, so you are. Jew, Catholic, Protestant. What a world! Look at that," Patryk said, pointing to the starry sky above. "That's where you'll find God. Not in some words in a book, not in some carving on an altar, and certainly not in the word of a man who thinks he can't be wrong. It's that—all that huge, mysterious thing up there!" Then he tapped his chest and added, "And that tiny mysterious thing inside here."

Chapter 31

THEY LEFT EARLY THE NEXT MORNING. THE SUN WAS JUST RISING, and a thin mist lay over the Wisła. As they headed out toward the center of the river, it was as if they were sailing through the clouds. Then, within minutes, the mist dispersed, and they settled down to the slow, gentle progress downstream.

The river was broad and calm, and Leo and Tomasz sat on the front float, watching the world slowly pass by. Farmers were out in the meadows, reaping the hay and piling it in neat stacks that glowed golden in the sunlight. A horse in a field suddenly bucked and galloped away, shaking its head, kicking up its heels, and trying to elude the flies buzzing around it. Clouds of midges hovered over the water.

They reached Mewe in the midafternoon and tied up on the bank below the large palace that towered on the hill above them.

"King Jan Sobieski built that for his wife, Marysienka," Patryk told them. "She was supposed to have been a real beauty. But I wager she wasn't a patch on the beauty I'm going to see. Zosia's a bit on the large size, but she's got the prettiest face. And anyway, I like a girl with a bit of meat on her!"

They walked up into the town and found that it was market day, so the streets were filled with people. Bel immediately wandered off to sniff around the stalls while they went to a café. Patryk ordered cakes and mugs of milk for them and a beer for himself. They sat at an outside table watching the bustle at the stalls, and Leo thought about the market in Nakel when Papa had tried to find work for them. Was Dorota still working in that tavern, and still being shouted at by that woman?

"Oh, well, mustn't keep Zosia waiting," Patryk said, finishing his beer and stretching like a lazy cat. He got up, ran his fingers through his glossy black hair, and fished some coins from his pocket. "Buy yourself some soused herring for tonight's meal. That man on the corner sells good ones, and if you go just before he packs up, he'll let you have them cheap. The bread rolls from that bakery opposite from his stall are a treat with the herring. I'll see you tomorrow morning—early, this time. I promise."

He strode off, waving to some traders he knew and smiling at all the young women he passed. Leo noticed that they all smiled back. Tomasz noticed too.

"Look at him," he said bitterly, "I bet there are kids up and down this river who don't even know he's their father."

"Don't you like him?" Leo asked, surprised.

"Of course I do, but he shouldn't go with girls and then run off and leave them—maybe with a baby to look after. That's what the count did to my mother, and it's not right."

Leo didn't say anything, and they sat in silence for a while.

They called Bel and then walked through the town, past the castle, and out onto the bluff overlooking the Wisła. A breeze was blowing up from the river, and a couple of boys were standing near the cliff's edge, preparing to fly their kite. The younger boy was holding the kite while the older one unwound a line that was wrapped around a stick.

"Right. On three, you let it go," the older one called. "One, two, three!"

The small boy let go, and the breeze immediately caught the kite and lifted it, higher and higher, until it was dancing in the blue sky above. The lad watched for a moment and then ran to stand next to the older boy, who turned and said something to him. The little boy nodded and the other one handed the stick and the line to him. A huge grin of delight broke out on his face as he took charge of the kite. The older boy looked down at him, smiled, and patted him on the shoulder.

"Do you think they're brothers?" Tomasz said.

"Probably."

There was a long pause while they watched the boys and the kite, then Tomasz said, "I always wanted a brother when I was growing up. My fath—the cobbler always joked that he'd buy me one if he became rich."

Another pause.

"And now I've got one," Tomasz said. "You."

Chapter 32

PATRYK WAS TRUE TO HIS WORD, AND HE ARRIVED BACK VERY early the next morning. The day had barely broken when he shook Leo and Tomasz awake. They rubbed their eyes and crawled out from under the canvas.

"Look at the river," Patryk said. "Must have stormed somewhere upstream. It's running fast, so we'll have our work cut out for us today. Here, I bought a couple of cakes for you. They'll give you strength, and you're going to need it. Eat up, and we'll get moving."

Compared to the previous days, it was a real battle to keep the raft on course. The river swirled and eddied unpredictably and there were sudden surges when the current rushed them forward. Patryk stood on the front float, sweep oar in hand, with his eyes fixed on the water ahead. Tomasz was at the back of the fourth float, using his pike as a rudder. Leo was on the third float, hurrying back and forth and plunging his pike into the water when Patryk wanted extra drag on one side or the other to keep the raft straight. It was tiring and hectic work, and there was no time for a break.

They swept past the entrance to the River Nogat, the raft rocking and jerking in the turbulent water as some of the stream headed off into the channel on the right. As soon as they'd passed the channel, the river calmed considerably, and even though they were still traveling fast, they could relax slightly. Patryk stopped barking out orders and gave them permission to lay down their pikes. Leo crossed onto the last float and sat side by side with Tomasz, their legs trailing in the river.

"I'm glad that's over," Tomasz said. "My arms were shaking like a newborn kitten trying to hold that pike straight. I hate all this water."

"We'll have to cross a lot more water to get to America," Leo pointed out.

"We'll be on a proper boat, not tree trunks like this. And once we get there, I swear I'm going to stay on solid ground."

Patryk called out the names of villages they floated past—Mosland, Grosse Schlanz, Kleine Schlanz—and then announced that if they kept up speed, they might make it all the way down to Dirschau by nightfall.

"He's probably got some other woman waiting for him!" Tomasz said.

"Probably," Leo chuckled, pleased that Tomasz had sounded amused rather than angry. "Have you ever liked a girl, Tom?"

"A sweetheart?" Tomasz said, grinning. "Well, not a proper one, but there was a girl I met in Posen. She was so pretty, and we kissed a couple of times."

"Real kissing?"

"It was real enough for me," Tomasz laughed, and his cheeks colored at the memory. "What about you?"

"Not really. Well, there was a girl when I was working at the manor last summer. She helped the cook. I liked her," Leo said, and a picture of Kassia came clearly into his mind. "She used to call me her 'little darling.'"

"Oooooh, Leo! How old was she?"

"Sixteen."

"Was she pretty?"

"Yes, she was," Leo said, and then laughed suddenly as a memory came back.

"What?" Tomasz asked.

"She tried to take my trousers down one time!"

"She did?" Tomasz asked, astonished. "Well, I would have let her!"

"No, it wasn't like that! I fell off a hay wagon and bruised myself. She rubbed some salve into my back and then started to undo my trousers to see if I had bruises farther down! But I wouldn't let her."

"Well, she could have rubbed my bum if she wanted. Then she could have turned me over and done the other side too!" Tomasz laughed. "Hey, in America, perhaps we'll find two sisters when we're older, and we'll fall in love and marry them. Wouldn't that just be the cream? We'd be real family then—real brothers."

He gave Leo a friendly punch, and Leo smiled and punched him back.

Bel stirred and stood up with a little whine, and Leo wondered if she thought they were fighting. Then he saw that she wasn't looking at them. She was staring at the river. She whined again, and the ruff at the back of her neck stood up.

He looked up and saw something that didn't make sense. Something was racing down the river toward them. Black objects appeared, and then disappeared in it. He gazed uncomprehendingly for a moment, and then realized—a churning, foaming wave was bearing down on them. The wave, over a meter high, was carrying branches and all kinds of flotsam with it.

Leo jumped to his feet and called, "Patryk! Look!"

Patryk looked back, and even from a distance, they could see the alarm on his face.

"Get your pikes!" he screamed.

Tomasz sprang to his feet and grabbed his pike, and Leo ran back up the float, jumped the gap, and picked up his.

"Leo! To starboard! I'll take the port!" Patryk yelled. "There's been a blockage somewhere upstream, and it's burst. We've got to keep the raft straight, or the wave'll tip us over. Tom, you hold her steady at the rear. Steady, steady. Here it comes. Hold on!"

The wave swept toward them. Leo saw it reach the fourth float and start to lift it. He thrust his pike into the water and pressed it hard against the side of the raft, gritting his teeth to hold it there as the wave rushed under his float.

Black branches, logs, and all kinds of rubbish rose and fell in the water as it whirled past him. He dug his toes into the trunk he was standing on, trying to keep his balance as the wave lifted the rear of his float and the trunks dipped downward. Down, down, and then, as the wave rolled toward the front, up and up.

There was a loud clunk as something hit the timbers under his feet. He glanced up and saw Patryk straining with his sweep oar as the wave passed under the first float. There was a grinding jolt as the raft struck something, and Leo slipped and fell. He crashed down, jarring his back, and almost lost his grip on his pike.

He scrambled up and saw that the wave had passed. The roaring, tumbling wall of water and branches was speeding away in front of them, leaving behind a calmer surface, where eddies and currents boiled up and then spread out in whirling rings.

Leo laughed out loud and turned to share his relief with Tomasz.

Tomasz's pike was lying across the tree trunks, but the back of the raft was empty.

Tomasz had gone.

Chapter 33

FOR A MOMENT, LEO COULDN'T TAKE IT IN. HE GLANCED AROUND to see if Tomasz was on one of the other floats, but there was only Patryk at the front, still staring at the retreating wave. He looked back again to where Tomasz should be. Nothing.

The realization chilled his spine and gripped his chest with terror.

He dropped his pike and ran. Ran to the gap. Jumped it. Ran down the tree trunks to the end of the raft. Skidded to a stop.

His eyes were wide and frantic, searching for a sign of Tomasz in the water. To the side. To the rear. To the other side.

Panic rose up in him. It can't be true. It will be all right. He'll be there. Any minute, he'll be there. He'll bob up, and the scare will be over. God, please. Please. Please.

The water was still boiling, swirling with movement stirred up by the wave. Bits of wood and weeds rose then sank again. Whirlpools spun and disappeared.

Leo couldn't breathe. His heart was pounding too fast. He opened his mouth and sucked in air.

There!

About twenty meters away.

A hand rose out of the water, and then sank.

"Tomasz," he said. He wanted to scream it but it came out as a tiny whisper.

He took a deep breath and dove into the brown, churning river.

He came to the surface and found himself in the grip of a powerful undertow that pulled him to the left, spun him around, and quickly dragged him away from the raft. He could hear barking, and as the river whirled him around, he saw Bel at the back of the raft. The water spun him again, and when he looked this time, Bel had gone. He caught a glimpse of her black-and-white head in the water. Then he struck out, swimming against the pull of the water toward the place where he'd seen the hand.

The river was so wide. The currents were so powerful. He glanced back at the raft. It was already so far away, as though still pulled by the speeding wave.

"Patryk!" he screamed.

He saw Patryk turn to look, but before he could call again, he was caught by a strong turbulence that pulled him under and twisted him upside down. He swallowed water and felt himself being spun and pulled sideways by an immense swirl. He fought against the vortex and came up to the surface, coughing and spluttering. The shore was closer, and he realized that he'd been swept away from where he'd been heading.

Bel bobbed up near him, dragged there by the same force that had carried him. She turned toward the shore and began paddling frantically for safety. He wanted to follow, but he struck out in the other direction, back to the middle of the river.

He had only swum a few strokes when he felt something hit him in the chest. A moment later, Tomasz's head shot out of the water right in front of him.

His eyes were wide, bloodshot, and terrified. The moment he saw Leo, he reached out and grabbed him.

"No!" Leo managed to say before Tomasz pulled himself tight

against him in panic, pinning his arms, and they both sank beneath the water.

Leo struggled to break the grip on his arms, but Tomasz simply held on tighter and they drifted deeper. Leo kicked frantically, and painfully, slowly, they rose again. For an instant, they broke the surface. Leo tried to gasp some air, but their weight took them under again, and he swallowed water instead.

He started to cough, and more water poured down his throat and into his lungs, choking him. He tried to swim using only his legs, but Tomasz seemed so heavy, and they were sinking deeper and deeper. He suddenly thought about that heavy belt around Tomasz's waist. If he could just get it off! But his arms were trapped. He frantically kicked his legs until they started to rise again. This time, when they reached the surface, he pounded Tomasz's ribs with his fists and managed to break his grip.

There was a look of terror on Tomasz's face as he tried to grab him again, but Leo swam backward out of his reach, and Tomasz sank below the water. Leo swam forward again, heading slightly to the side, and then dove under and grabbed his friend's shoulders from behind.

Leo wrapped his arms around Tomasz from the back and kicked and kicked with his legs until he managed to pull them up from the depths and into the air again. This time, he was in control. He kept one arm around Tomasz's chest and grabbed his chin with his other hand. He lay back in the water, panting for air, and heard Tomasz doing the same. If he could just keep him calm and lighten the weight, he might be able to swim on his back and pull them both to safety.

"All right," he gasped. "You're all right."

He felt Tomasz relax, but already the weight was starting to pull them lower in the water.

"Belt," Leo said, frantically thrashing his legs to keep them afloat. "Take…belt…off."

He moved his hand down from Tomasz's chest toward that heavy belt. He touched it and found the clasp.

"Take…off," he repeated, trying to keep his mouth above water.

Tomasz started to struggle. His hand came down and grasped Leo's, ripping the fingers away from the belt.

"No…America," Tomasz said, his voice a hoarse whisper.

"Got…to," Leo managed to splutter, before the struggle took them under again.

They sank deeper and deeper, and Leo fumbled for the clasp of the belt while Tomasz writhed and pushed to keep his hand away. Then Tomasz's elbow suddenly drove back into Leo's face, cracking straight onto the bridge of his nose. Leo jerked away in shock, and he lost hold of Tomasz. He reached out, but grabbed only water. The next moment, freed from Tomasz's weight, he shot up to the surface.

He took a huge gasp of air and dove down. He opened his eyes, but the water was so churned with mud, he could see nothing. He swam in one direction, feeling all around him, and then back in another direction. Then he swam deeper, around and around, until finally he could hold his breath no longer, and he burst up into the air again.

Twice more he dove down, each time more frantically. But the third time he came up to breathe, he knew he couldn't go back down again.

He looked across the water.

Something rose briefly to the surface about forty meters downstream close to the shore. Could it have been floating hair? He struck out after it, pounding his arms into the water until his strokes grew weaker and he realized he was just being borne along by the current. He made feeble movements to head for the shore, but a terrible exhaustion paralyzed his limbs. He rolled onto his back and lay there, waiting to sink.

But he didn't sink. Lying limply in the water, his arms out to the side, he was swept along like a piece of driftwood. Through half-closed eyes, he watched the sky move above him as he floated downstream. His mind was blank, and he felt nothing except coldness and a vague yearning to let go and slide away from everything. It would be so easy, like turning over into darkness. All that kept him from that collapse were the clouds. They were so pretty—huge, soft, rolling whiteness against the blue. He wanted to close his eyes, wanted the release of sleep. It was there, by his side—inviting. All he had to do was let go, but those clouds…

There was no time. No sound. He lost the feel of water, of himself. It was all merging together. There were just the clouds and little patches of blue. And smooth movement.

Then, muffled, far away—a noise.

His brain stirred, trying to make sense of it. Trying to remember.

The noise again.

It was…a bark.

There was water in his ears. He was in the river. He was floating. He might drown. He had to move. He could drown.

He dragged his eyes away from the clouds and rolled his head toward the sound. There was the riverbank. A tree moved across his vision, and there, next to it, was Bel. She was standing on the bank. Her whole body was jerking with her barks.

Why couldn't he hear them? Water in his ears?

He lifted his head and caught a glimpse of Patryk running along the bank. Then the movement of his head unbalanced him, and he felt his legs sinking. The water closed over him. He struggled feebly, but when he tried to pull air into his lungs, there was just water rushing in. He couldn't stop it. He let go.

There was a bump against his shoulder, and then a strong hand gripped his arm and jerked him to the surface. Another arm closed around his chest, crushing him, and water rose up from his lungs, spewing out. He was coughing. More water spewed from him. He was being hauled, carried, and squeezed toward the bank. He was lifted up and thrown onto the grass.

His stomach heaved, and more water vomited out of his mouth. Patryk was by his side, pressing down on his back until he stopped coughing and could take a huge breath—and another, and another, until his lungs stopped burning and his eyes cleared. He could see the details of the blades of grass next to his face.

"Oh, thank God," Patryk said as Leo rolled over. "I thought you were gone too."

Leo lay for a moment, thinking about that sentence.

"Tomasz?" he finally asked.

Patryk reached down and lifted him into a sitting position. He kept his arms wrapped around him as he spoke. "He's dead, Leo. I found him facedown in the water. His waistcoat was snagged on an overhanging branch. I tried…I tried, but I just couldn't get him breathing again. There was nothing I could do. I'm sorry."

Leo heard the words, but they didn't seem to change anything. They were just words. They weren't real. They didn't make Tomasz dead. Perhaps it was a mistake.

"Take me," he said.

Patryk stood and picked him up so easily. He slung him across his back, and Leo slipped his arms around his neck. He could feel the warmth of Patryk's body and the ripple of muscles as he walked, and he was a little child again, being given a piggyback ride by Papa.

Bel ran ahead and then stopped and sat down next to a bundle on the bank ahead. She lifted her head and howled. And Leo knew that it was Tomasz.

He slid from Patryk's back. On trembling legs, he stumbled the last few paces and then sank down at the side of the bundle. Patryk had covered Tomasz's face with the soaking waistcoat. Gently, Leo lifted it off and looked.

Tomasz's face was deathly white. His lips were blue, and his eyes were wide open in that same terrible expression of fear Leo had seen in the water. He closed the eyelids and bent down and kissed the chilly forehead. As he sat back up, he pulled Tomasz's body with him.

And there, cradling the unresponsive corpse in his arms, it became real. Tomasz was gone. He would never come back.

And there, at last, Leo began to weep for his lost friend.

Chapter 34

Patryk carried Tomasz back downstream to where the log raft was tied up. Leo walked a few steps behind, not wanting to look at Tomasz's white face and the drips of water still running from his hair. Suddenly his thin arm slipped down, and Leo couldn't take his eyes off it as it swayed from side to side. The blue veins in the wrist, the long fingers, slightly curled, and that patch of mud on the forearm. Back and forth the arm swung, in rhythm with Patryk's stride.

They gently laid Tomasz in the center of the second float and covered his face with the waistcoat again. Leo helped push the raft away from the bank and then, as it reached the middle of the river and glided steadily downstream on the current, he went back and sat next to Tomasz. Bel was lying beside the body and she got up and placed her muzzle on Leo's lap, looking up at him mournfully. He caressed her head and she settled down with a sigh.

It was comforting to stroke her.

For a long time, he stared blankly at the passing countryside until the light thickened and night started to fall.

"Leo, can you give me a hand, please?" Patryk's voice broke into his trance, and he saw that they were coming in to land.

He stumbled to his feet, feeling exhausted, and slowly made his way to the front of the raft. Ahead of them, the lights of a town rose up the slope. In the gloom, he saw the silhouette of what looked like the round turrets of a castle floating mysteriously above the river.

"What's that?" Leo asked, not believing his eyes.

"This is Dirschau," Patryk said. "And that's the famous railway bridge. Amazing looking thing, isn't it? Grab your pike, Leo, and let's get ashore."

By the time they'd secured the raft for the night, it was totally dark and Patryk decided that they would have to wait until the following morning to deal with Tomasz's body.

"The priests will be in their beds by now. Best to have a bit of food and sleep down here. You get the camp set up while I light a fire."

Leo tied the rope between two trees, spread the canvas across it, and then staked the sides out like a tent. He sat down and stared at the flames dancing on the fire. His whole being felt empty and tired, and he just wanted to slip into sleep. But Patryk made him eat some bread and herring before he let him crawl away to the tent and lie down.

He closed his eyes and drifted straight into a terrible dream. Tomasz's body was lying on the raft, and rats were climbing out of the water and running all over him.

He jerked out of the dream and sat bolt upright in shock. Patryk was outside the tent, sitting in the flickering glow of the fire.

"We can't leave him on the raft!" Leo called, his voice cracking in panic.

"Of course not. I brought him here," Patryk said, pointing to the shadowy shape on the ground next to him. "I've wrapped him in canvas, and I'll be with him all night. Bel and I will look after him. Don't you fret. Just lie down and get some sleep. There's a good lad."

Sometime later Leo woke again to a chugging, slapping sound in the dark and he saw lights moving on the river.

"What is it?" he mumbled, still half asleep.

"It's just a paddle steamer," Patryk said. He was still there next to the fire with Bel by his side, sitting guard over Tomasz as he'd promised. "Go back to sleep, Leo."

Patryk was gone from early morning until nearly noon, and Leo sat waiting for him, numbly watching the boats coming and going on the river. Trains puffed over the railway bridge, and he couldn't stop thinking about how they'd tried to catch the train from Bromberg. If only Tomasz hadn't been so intent on keeping all the money for America, they could have bought tickets to Danzig, and he would be alive now.

He pulled aside the canvas, making sure that it didn't uncover Tomasz's face, and looked at the belt wrapped around his waist. That heavy belt had dragged him underwater. That heavy belt had killed him. He had dreamed of using the money to build a new life in America, but the dream had killed him. Leo stared at the belt, and he hated the money inside.

Patryk came back with a small handcart that he'd borrowed. He explained that he'd been delayed at the police station.

"The priest told me that I had notify the police of the death first. But they weren't really interested. They just kept me waiting for hours. Then they asked a few questions and made me sign a statement. Anyway, we've got the necessary papers now."

They placed Tomasz on the handcart and wheeled him along the riverbank toward the town. Bel followed for a while, but Patryk ordered her to stay, and she obediently trotted back and sat down near the raft. They made their way into the town and crossed the busy square. The cart jolted and shook on the cobblestones, and the canvas slid off Tomasz's feet. An old lady glanced at them and crossed herself.

They finally stopped in front of a church where bells were ringing from the top of its tall brick tower.

"This is it, the Church of the Holy Cross Elevation," Patryk said. "I asked at another one, St. Stanislaw Kostka, but that's Protestant. It makes no difference to me because I've got no time for any of them, but I chose this one because I know you're a Catholic."

"Yes, but Tom isn't," Leo said. "He's a Jew."

"Of course! You're right. Oh, well, we'd better find out if they have a synagogue in this town."

They walked back toward the square and came across a large, red-faced man who was dismounting from his horse.

"Can you tell me if there's a synagogue here in Dirschau, my friend?" Patryk asked him.

"You're no friend of mine if you're a Jew," the man snapped, tying his horse's reins to a metal ring on the wall of a house.

"No Jew," Patryk said calmly. "Just asking if there's a synagogue."

But the man simply ignored him. He spat noisily onto the ground, gave his horse a slap on the rump, and walked up the steps and into the house.

"That's religions for you," Patryk muttered. "They hate each other like poison. A plague on all of them, I say."

They asked another three men who said they didn't know, and then an old woman sweeping the road in front of her house told them that, yes, there was a synagogue in town. She gave them directions to find it.

The synagogue was empty when they arrived, but the address of Rabbi Jakub Zohn was written on the board outside it. The house was just around the corner from the synagogue, and the rabbi's wife answered their knock. She looked past them at the canvas bundle in the handcart and gave a little sigh.

"A child?" she asked.

"A drowned lad," Patryk nodded.

"Poor mite. Wheel him around the back into the courtyard, and I'll call the rabbi."

Chapter 35

RABBI ZOHN WAS A TALL, STOOPED, GRIZZLED OLD MAN WITH piercing black eyes. Leo found him rather intimidating, but surprisingly, Patryk got on with him from the start.

The rabbi walked over to the cart and lifted the canvas. He looked at Tomasz for a long time before turning and asking, "He's a Jewish boy?"

"Ah, that's a long story," Patryk replied. "Leo can explain."

Leo told him that Tomasz's mother was Jewish, but when he tried to explain about the tailor and the count, he got increasingly tongue-tied and finally fell silent under the rabbi's intense stare. Patryk took over and explained how they had met up and had come down the River Weichsel on a log raft.

"So you're a raft rider, eh?" the rabbi said, his eyes lighting up. "My father was a woodsman up in Galicia, and when I was young, I always used to look at the men who floated the logs downstream and wish I could go with them. Come in, come in, both of you. My wife will make tea for us."

They went into the house, and Leo stayed in the kitchen with the rabbi's wife while the rabbi took Patryk off to his study. Mrs. Zohn pointed to a seat at the big kitchen table, and Leo sat there and watched while she boiled the water on the stove and made the tea, bringing out fine china for the men and a bowl for Leo.

"You'll be hungry," she said, but Leo shook his head. "I'll put these little cakes here for you anyway."

She took the men's tea into the study and then came back into the kitchen. She began cutting up vegetables and putting them into a big pot on the stove, where a chicken was simmering. Leo looked at her, quietly working away at her tasks. From time to time, she glanced at him and smiled gently.

"Try one. I made them myself," she said, nodding at the plate of cakes. He wasn't hungry, but he took one out of politeness and ate it, breaking off small pieces of the sweet, crumbly pastry and washing them down with sips of tea.

"Tell me about your friend," she said, stirring the pot.

Her back was to him, so he found it easier to talk. Once he'd started, he didn't stop, even when she left her cooking and came and sat at the table, listening intently to every word. He told her everything he knew, only leaving out the part about the killing of the man who'd tried to steal the money. When he described how Tomasz had fallen into the river, she reached over and took Leo's hand, holding it in hers and stroking it, and not letting go even when he finally finished speaking.

Leo felt drained after reliving it all, and he was glad that Mrs. Zohn didn't ask any questions but was content to sit silently with him at the table. They were still there when, a few minutes later, the door opened and the rabbi came in. He bent down and whispered in his wife's ear and then went back toward the study.

"My husband has agreed to bury Tomasz in our cemetery. The funeral will be tomorrow morning, but he's asked me to perform the taharah. It's a ceremony where we wash the body and prepare it for burial. There's another woman, Esther, who always comes to help me, but I wonder if you would like to do it with us."

Leo's heart lurched with fear. He withdrew his hand from hers and shook his head.

"I know it sounds terrible, but it really is not," Mrs. Zohn said kindly. "I think you might even find it a comfort. We call it the Last Kindness. You, who were such a good friend to him, might wish to do this last kindness for him."

"No!" Leo said, shaking his head vigorously.

"I understand. It's not an easy thing, and you look very tired, child. The men sound as if they will talk until evening. Why don't you rest for a while."

She showed him to a small bedroom upstairs, and he lay on the bed. She covered him with a blanket and left him to sleep.

When he awoke, he heard movements down in the yard. He looked out of the open window and saw Mrs. Zohn and another woman fetching buckets of water from the pump. Tomasz, covered with a white sheet, was lying on a trestle table. His clothes were neatly folded on a chair. The two women put down the buckets and stood solemnly at the head of the table.

"Tomasz," Mrs. Zohn said, speaking to him as if he could hear, "Esther and I ask your permission to perform a taharah on you. We ask your forgiveness for any disruption we might cause you, and for any error we might make."

They stood silently for a moment. Then they moved to Tomasz's right side and began to wash him. Mrs. Zohn washed his face, while Esther rolled down the sheet a little and began cleaning his right shoulder and the right side of his chest.

They worked slowly and reverently, and it seemed so right and proper that Tomasz should be treated like this—to be cleaned by such gentle, loving hands. Leo suddenly knew he had to join them. He had to give his friend this last kindness.

Chapter 36

Mrs. Zohn didn't look surprised when Leo stepped up next to her and asked if he could help. She smiled and brushed his cheek with her hand.

"I know he will be pleased. Go and wash your hands under the pump first."

The water ran cold and clear from the pump, and he scrubbed until his hands were clean. He looked down at the pink aliveness of his fingers and a moment of doubt ran through him. Could he touch dead flesh? Yes, he could. Mrs. Zohn had spoken to Tomasz as if he were still alive. She had said that he would be pleased, as if he were still here and not gone yet.

Mrs. Zohn gave him a small pointed stick. "When Esther has finished washing his hand, I would like you to clean the dirt from his fingernails and then cut them with those scissors."

Leo stood, waiting, and when Esther moved away to begin washing the right leg, he stepped in and took hold of Tomasz's hand. It was cold, and when he held the first finger, it felt stiff and very dead. He wasn't repulsed and he didn't let go, but he couldn't believe that Tomasz was still there. He shivered slightly and then slipped the point of the stick under the fingernail and began scraping out the dirt.

He worked methodically, and soon all feelings of fear and uncertainty left him. It was a service he could do for the friend he had known, the friend who had lived in this empty shell, and he wanted to do it well.

When the nails were clean, he cut them with the scissors. Then he did the same for the right foot.

By this time, the women were cleaning Tomasz from his waist down to his groin, and Leo kept his eyes turned away, embarrassed that the women were seeing his friend's private parts. Would they say something about him not being circumcised? Would it mean that he couldn't be buried in a Jewish cemetery? When he glanced at them, he saw the same calm, gentle respect on their faces, and as soon as they had finished, they rolled the sheet up to cover Tomasz's nakedness.

Mrs. Zohn told Leo to wash himself again, and then he dealt with the nails on the left hand and then the left foot. When he finished, the three of them washed their hands once more and then filled the buckets with water from the pump. Mrs. Zohn removed the sheet from Tomasz and threw the water all over his body. Esther and Mrs. Zohn chanted, "You are pure…You are pure…You are pure." Then they fetched towels and dried him, and asked Leo to comb his hair. They laid small pieces of broken pottery over Tomasz's eyes and mouth before covering him entirely with a new sheet.

"Usually, we would dress him now," Mrs. Zohn said, "but I want to wash his clothes first, so I'll put them on him tomorrow morning before the burial." She turned to Tomasz and spoke to him. "Forgive us for breaking the ritual, and excuse any errors we may have committed in the performance of the taharah."

The three of them lifted the trestle table and carried Tomasz toward a small shed on the other side of the courtyard. They placed the table inside the shed so Tomasz's feet were pointing toward the door. Mrs. Zohn lit a candle and set it down near his head.

"My husband will come here later and again tomorrow morning to recite psalms, and Esther and I will take turns to stay with Tomasz all through the night, so he will be well taken care of. For the moment, we can leave him. Now we will walk backward out the door, all the time facing Tomasz. That's right."

Leo stepped back into the courtyard, and Mrs. Zohn closed the door of the shed. It was twilight, and he caught a glimpse of the first star in the purple sky. Then an aching fatigue overcame him, and he began to tremble.

Patryk was talking with Rabbi Zohn on the steps outside the kitchen door, but as soon as he saw Leo, he came across and put his arm around his shoulder.

"You look all-in, lad. Come on. Let's go back to the raft and get some rest."

Chapter 37

PATRYK AND LEO SAID GOOD-BYE TO RABBI AND MRS. ZOHN AND made their way back down toward the river.

"That rabbi. What a talker!" Patryk chuckled. "There's nothing I don't know about his life! But he's a good chap, as wise as they come. He's been through some rough times, I can tell you, but there's not a bitter bone in his body. Oh, look who's coming."

Bel came racing up the hill toward them, barking with excitement, and jumped up at Leo, nearly knocking him over. When they got back to their little camp, Patryk began to cook some soup. Leo sat down and Bel slumped across his feet, as if to make sure that he couldn't leave her alone again.

The heat of the day had quickly evaporated as night had fallen, and the soup was warming and tasty. When they finished eating, they sat silently watching the lights of the boats passing on the river until Leo said he was going to bed.

"Oh, this is for you," Patryk said pulling something from under his waistcoat and giving it to him. It was Tomasz's belt. "Mrs. Zohn gave it to me when she took it off Tom. She said it was heavy, as if there was something in it. I felt it—it's money isn't it?"

Leo nodded. "I hate it. I don't want it. Let them bury it with Tom. It's cursed."

"Money's not cursed, Leo."

"It killed him!"

"The river killed Tomasz, not this money. Is the river cursed? Is the water cursed?"

"I don't want it."

"You might not want it, but you need it. We need it. Someone's got to pay for Tom's funeral tomorrow. I was going to sell some of these logs, but I'm not going to do that if there's money—money that you're prepared to see buried in a grave. What good will that do? What about your parents? You said you ran away to get money for your family. Well, send them some of this. What about your journey to America? How are you going to pay for that if this money's in the grave? Of all the people in the world, Tom would have wanted you to have it."

"I don't want it," Leo said, throwing the belt on the ground and going into the tent.

He lay down, covered himself with a blanket, and tried to forget. But all he could see when he closed his eyes was Tomasz. Not the dead Tomasz he had helped wash today, but his living, smiling, and hopeful friend who had talked so excitedly about the future and what they would do with the money.

The next morning, he got up just before dawn. Patryk was still sleeping, but Bel woke and wagged her tail at the prospect of a walk.

A mist was covering the riverbank as they walked together, and it felt as if they were moving through the clouds. Away in the distance, he could hear the muffled noises from the boats coming and going in the port. A chilly wind started to blow, and the mist cleared. There was the river, running quietly and steadily.

Patryk was right. The river wasn't cursed. It was just flowing water. And the money? It was just metal—not cursed at all. He would use it to pay for the funeral, and because he didn't know where Tomasz's mother and the cobbler lived, he would send some home to his own family.

Patryk was working on the raft when Leo got back, so he went into the tent and cut a few of the stitches along the edge of the belt—those stitches so carefully sewn by Tomasz—and slid out one of the big silver coins. It really was heavy, and he wondered how much it was worth.

"A lot," Patryk said when Leo asked him. He took the coin and felt its weight. "I'm not sure how much, because I've never seen one of these before, but this is good silver. It will certainly be enough to cover the cost of the funeral, and perhaps even a headstone too. I'm glad you've changed your mind. Now come on. Let's smarten ourselves up to say good-bye to Tom."

Chapter 38

THE CEMETERY WAS A FLAT, DESOLATE PIECE OF GROUND ON THE outskirts of town. A low wall ran around it and a couple of twisted blackthorn bushes stood in one corner, shaking in the strong, cold wind.

"It will be all right," Leo kept saying to himself as he and Patryk walked side by side, following the cart on which the coffin lay. "It will be all right."

They tied Bel to a post outside the cemetery. The driver held the horse steady as Leo and Patryk slid the rough pine coffin from the back of the cart. They carried it through the gateway to where the rabbi, Mrs. Zohn, and Esther were waiting, and the five of them walked toward the grave.

The gravedigger was standing beside the hole he had dug. As they approached, he laid out two lengths of rope on the ground and indicated they should put the coffin on top of them.

Rabbi Zohn removed the lid of the coffin. Then, he stood back and began to recite in Hebrew. Leo didn't want to see into the coffin, so he stared into the distance at the solid gray clouds above the town. But when the rabbi stopped chanting, he forced himself to look. There lay Tomasz, dressed neatly in his clean clothes. His skin was paler than ever and seemed waxy, as though he were turning to marble.

The rabbi slowly folded the top of the shroud down, covering Tomasz's face, and Leo knew he would never see him again.

The lid was put back on the coffin, and the gravedigger nailed it down while Rabbi Zohn chanted another psalm. The gravedigger picked up one end of the ropes and signaled Patryk to pick up the other. They strained to lift the coffin, swung it over the hole, and slowly lowered it into the ground. Everyone took a step closer to the edge of the grave and peered down as the coffin settled on the bottom of the grave. The gravedigger twitched the ropes free and hauled them up again.

"It is usual for someone to deliver the hesped, a few words honoring the deceased," Rabbi Zohn said. "Patryk, would you say something?"

Patryk look startled and embarrassed, but he cleared his throat. "Tom was a good worker…" he began, and then seemed lost. He cleared his throat again. "He was…he didn't like the water…but he was brave, and I was proud to have him as a raft rider with me."

He looked around helplessly, not sure how to go on, and Leo knew he would have to take over.

"Tomasz was my friend," he said, fighting to stop the sob that was rising at the back of his throat. "He helped me. He looked after me when I was…alone."

He could feel his jaw begin to tremble, and his eyes filled with tears. But he would not let them fall. He would not. He clenched his jaw tightly to stop the trembling, and then forced himself to go on.

"He was the best friend I've ever had. He was kind…and funny. He made me laugh when I was sad. And he sang songs—he could make them up himself. And he was a good person. Bad things happened to him, and he did some bad things, but it wasn't his fault. God knows that. He was a good person. A good person."

He looked up, his eyes blazing, challenging anyone to deny

what he had said. But all he saw were kind faces looking at him, nodding in silent agreement.

"And I won't ever forget him. Ever," he managed to add before those tears finally slid from his eyes and down his cheeks.

Rabbi Zohn gave a sign and the gravedigger began shoveling the earth into the grave with the back of his spade.

The first clods of earth rattled and thudded on the coffin, but soon the wooden box was hidden, and there was the near silence of earth falling on earth.

Chapter 39

I T STARTED DURING THE NIGHT.

Leo opened his eyes, not knowing where he was. Moonlight was pouring through the window.

He was in a bed.

In a room.

He blinked and thought. Yes, he was in Rabbi Zohn's house. This was the little bedroom that overlooked the courtyard. They had come back to the house for a meal after the funeral. Patryk and the rabbi had talked all evening, so Mrs. Zohn had said they could spend the night there.

Yes, there was Patryk asleep on a mattress near the window. Bel was on the floor next to him.

Leo shivered and pulled the blanket up around him. His mouth was dry, and there was a gurgling in his stomach. A sudden spasm in his guts made him sit up in pain. He clenched his teeth, and the pain gradually ebbed away. He lay down. His guts gurgled again, and the skin on his face crawled and tightened. Supposing he needed the privy? Would he be able to find his way through the dark, unfamiliar house?

Twice more during the night, he was dragged awake by a stabbing pain in his gut, but each time it eased and he sank back into sleep. Shortly after dawn, Patryk shook him and told him it was time to go. When he stood up, his legs felt heavy, and when he kneeled down to tie the laces of his boots, the blood rushed to his head and made the room spin.

The rabbi was leaving to take an early service at the synagogue, so they said good-bye to him first and then went into the kitchen. Patryk sat down to drink a coffee with Mrs. Zohn. The smell of it made Leo feel sick, so he went outside. The early morning air was cool, and he shivered as he leaned against the courtyard wall. Bel stood at his feet, wagging her tail in anticipation of getting moving, but Leo didn't even have the strength to bend down to give her an encouraging pat.

At last, Patryk came out with Mrs. Zohn. They thanked her, said good-bye, and then set off toward the river. Leo felt as if he were in a daze, unable to do anything more than concentrate on keeping his legs moving in step with Patryk's.

They reached the riverbank and were walking toward the raft when Leo doubled up with a searing, urgent pain in his gut. There was no time to hide behind a tree or a bush, and no time for embarrassment. He barely had time to pull his trousers down and squat before the contents of his bowels emptied in a watery gush. He swayed and almost fell backward into the mess. He struggled to stand up, but another spasm hit him, driving him to his knees as the foul-smelling liquid splattered down his thighs and onto his trousers.

He crawled forward, trying to get to the river to wash himself, but Patryk had already run to the raft and fetched a bucket of water.

"Stay still," Patryk said, and he sluiced water across Leo's buttocks and legs. "Now, let's get those trousers off, and I'll wash them."

"I'm sorry," Leo said, through chattering teeth.

"No need to be sorry. Come on. Can you stand?"

Patryk helped him to his feet.

"I'm all right," Leo said, shrugging Patryk's arm from around his shoulders.

All he wanted to do was get to the raft and cover himself with something—get away from here, and this shameful moment. He took about ten steps, feeling that it was all over, and then his bowels convulsed again. He crouched down as more watery muck poured out of him. This time, when he tried, he couldn't stand on his own. Patryk half carried, half dragged him the rest of the way to their camp and laid him inside the tent.

"You're burning up," Patryk said, covering him with a blanket.

Leo couldn't speak. It felt as if he had lost control of his body. Huge shudders swept through him, chattering his teeth and shaking his body, and stuff oozed out of his bowels. How could there be so much liquid inside him? Was it blood?

"We've got to get you to a doctor," Patryk said, lifting him and tucking the blanket around him.

"I can't…help it," Leo managed to say.

"Don't be silly," Patryk said, swinging him up over his shoulder.

There was another explosion from his gut, and Leo stopped fighting it. A terrible weakness ran through him, and he felt entirely helpless. He was half aware of being carried, but he no longer knew where to, or why.

Sometime later, there were voices. He knew that he was not outside. He wasn't being carried anymore. Someone was lifting his body. Wiping him. Washing him. He made out the word "doctor." But he didn't care. This pain, this shivering, this exhaustion—this must be dying. Soon it would be over. He would be released. Somewhere far away, he felt his bowels move again. What was coming out?

Cold hands were touching him. Poking into his armpit and into his groin. Feeling around his neck. Opening his mouth. He tried to concentrate, to see, but his eyes wouldn't focus. Was he going blind? A deep, booming voice nearby, saying words. Too loud. The sounds hurt him. Then, one word. His brain grabbed it out of the jumble of meaningless sounds, heard it clearly, held on to it, sent it running through the echoey darkness inside his head—"cholera."

Later, much later. Patryk's voice. But he couldn't listen. He had to ask.

"Am...I...dying?" he managed to whisper.

"No. You must drink."

He felt himself lifted into a sitting position but his head lolled helplessly forward.

"Drink," the voice commanded, and something hard rattled against his teeth. Liquid seeped into his mouth—a strange sweet, salty taste. He swallowed. Then again. And again.

He was lying down. The spasms again. The sticky, wet feeling around his buttocks.

He was being held up, and the liquid was poured into him again. This time, he couldn't keep it down and it surged up out of his mouth.

Voices. Hands. Something going down his throat.

Choking him.

His stomach filling. Cramps. His bowels emptying.

His stomach filling. Cramps. His bowels emptying.

Until he could bear no more.

Chapter 40

HE FELT THE SUNSHINE ON HIS FACE, AND HE OPENED HIS EYES to its yellow blaze. Then he had to shut them again—too late. The light had started a terrible pounding in his head. He summoned all his strength to raise his hand and let it fall across his eyes to cut out the glare.

"Leo?" said a woman's voice. "Are you awake?"

He tried to speak but it came out in a mumble. There was the sound of closing curtains and the glaring light went away. He slowly opened his eyes and saw Mrs. Zohn at the window. She smiled at him as she came toward the bed and sat down.

"Ah, you're back with us. I tell you, child, there were times when we thought we'd lost you. You were so ill—in a coma for three days. But Dr. Goldszmit performed miracles. He came four times a day to treat you, making sure that you were getting enough liquids. 'Salt, sugar, and water,' he kept telling me. 'It's the only way to treat cholera.' And he was right. We had to put a tube down your throat to pour the mixture into you, poor mite. You must be sore."

Leo tried swallowing, and his throat rasped painfully. He nodded.

"I've got some good chicken soup on the stove. That will ease the soreness and bring your strength back," she said, getting up. "I'll bring you a bowl."

"Patryk…" he whispered hoarsely.

"He's gone, Leo," she said gently. "He stayed as long as he could.

He was terribly worried about you. But he just had to deliver that timber to Danzig."

She left the room, and suddenly a gray hopelessness filled him. Tomasz was gone. Patryk was gone. He was alone again. He couldn't go on.

He turned over and closed his eyes. When Mrs. Zohn came back with the soup, he pretended he was asleep. He didn't want to eat. He didn't want to listen to her talking. He just wanted to go to sleep and never wake up. Eventually, she went away.

The next time she came into the room, he was lying there, staring at the ceiling, and he didn't even bother to pretend to be asleep. She offered the bowl of soup to him, but he said nothing, made no movement.

"Please, Leo, you must eat," she said, but he didn't move his eyes from the big crack in the ceiling.

Night came. He slept and woke, and slept and woke.

The morning came.

He felt empty. He had no feeling. He was just a pair of eyes looking out at a bleak world he didn't want to see.

Mrs. Zohn came with a bowl of milk. He looked at her and then looked away. She spoke gently and kindly and tried to get him to say something, but he was somewhere else, miles away, in a cold space where she couldn't touch him.

She went away.

Time passed.

"Leo, this is Dr. Goldszmit," Mrs. Zohn said.

The black-bearded man leaned down and peered at him with his deep blue eyes. He didn't speak, simply began to prod Leo— around the neck, in his armpits, in his groin. He laid his hand across his forehead to check his temperature and then held his wrist to feel his pulse. He examined his fingernails, pulled his mouth open, drew his eyelids down, tapped his chest, crossed his legs and struck him just below his knee, and peered into his ears.

"No diarrhea?" Dr. Goldszmit asked.

Mrs. Zohn shook her head.

"Then the cholera has passed. I can find nothing wrong with his body. The effect of the fever? The coma? I can't tell."

They moved away and out of the room. They closed the door, and he could hear their voices. No words—but he knew they were talking about him. He didn't care. He wanted to be dead. Dead, like Tomasz.

It was evening when Rabbi Zohn came into the room. The light was thickening, and Leo could hardly make out his features as he pulled up a chair and sat in the shadow by the side of the bed. The rabbi said nothing, and the silence stretched for so long that Leo's mind began to slip away, back to the place where he thought about nothing.

"What is it, boy?" The rabbi's voice was soft, but it still startled Leo when it came. "I know you have been ill, and you have been through terrible things, but you cannot give up now. You have to endure, Leo."

Leo's throat thickened at the word. Endure. He remembered Papa saying it in that same quiet way. There was a softening around his eyes, as if tears might come, and then an aching weariness sucked at him. No, he couldn't go on.

"You have to endure," the rabbi repeated, as if he guessed the power of the word. "But you must know that already. I have no idea of your life, but a boy of your age, on his own, leaving his country to go to another—such a boy has not had an easy life. Yet you got this far. You overcame the difficulties. You endured."

The rabbi leaned forward. Leo tried to concentrate on looking at the ceiling and the crack that was becoming almost invisible in the fading light, but that soft voice could not be ignored.

"I will not lie to you. Life will continue to throw difficulties at you—sorrows, pain, and disappointment. It does to everybody. And things you want to last forever will change and slip out of your grasp. People you love will leave you, or die, like poor Tomasz. There will be times when you will feel you cannot go on, but you will find the strength. I know you will. And though life can be hard, there are all the fine things too: beautiful things, funny things. And, best of all, there is love. But to enjoy these things you have to be fully alive to the good and to the bad. Some people aren't fully alive. They are beaten down by the difficulties, and they become bitter, or numb. They cannot bear the pain, so they close up and put a shell around themselves. They cut out the pain, but they cut out the joy too. Don't do that, Leo. I want you to endure, and live through the bad and enjoy the good. Endure, Leo. You can. You are strong. You have come this far. You can go on. And on."

The rabbi laid his hand on Leo's head, and then got up and left the room.

He dreamed about the family. They were all there. Papa, and Mama, and all his brothers and sisters, even the twins—all of them toiling in a huge field that stretched to the horizon. They were stooped over, trying to dig up a crop from the ground. Potatoes? He didn't know because, for all their frantic scratching in the soil, they were finding nothing. Their fingernails were torn and bleeding. Sweat poured from them. But they kept going, on and on, uncomplaining, moving away from him across the immense field.

Dr. Goldszmit came the following morning, and he was not alone. A tall, slender girl with long black hair followed him into the room. It was obvious that she was the doctor's daughter—she had the same high cheekbones, and the same large blue eyes, except hers were even more startling and beautiful because there was a violet tinge to them. For a moment, he was scared that she would watch while he was examined, but Dr. Goldszmit said, "Klara," and nodded at the window. She walked over and stood there, studiously staring out at the courtyard.

"Feeling better, I see," said Dr. Goldszmit when he finished prodding and checking.

Leo almost replied, almost said yes, but then he turned his eyes away. At the same time, he realized how foolish he felt. Yes, he was feeling better. He had woken up with more hope and energy than he had for days, but he didn't want to admit it.

"Good," Dr. Goldszmit said, as if Leo had replied. "Klara, are you coming?"

She turned around from the window and followed her father to the door, but the whole time she was looking at Leo. There was an amused smile on her lips, as if she knew everything about him and she found it funny. An embarrassed blush rose to his cheeks. She closed the door, and he wanted to see her again. At once.

It was nearly half an hour before he did. There was a frantic clicking noise on the floorboards outside his door. The door opened, and Bel came dashing in, wagging her tail in such excitement that her whole rear end moved from side to side. The sight of her brought a rush of joy to his heart, and he sat up. She put her front paws on the bed and began licking his hand.

"Oh, Bel," he said, leaning forward and cuddling her. "I've missed you."

"I knew you could talk."

He looked up. Klara was standing in the doorway.

Embarrassed but pleased to see her, he concentrated on scratching Bel's head and trying to avoid her lunging attempts to lick his face.

Klara crossed the room and sat on the bed. "Do you talk to people too, or only to dogs?" she asked. She began patting Bel's back, and then she turned those astonishing, amused eyes on him. "Well? Do you?"

"Yes," he said, unable to stop a silly, shy smile from coming to his lips.

"Oh, good," Klara said. Then, instead of talking, she made a fuss about Bel, stroking her and laughing when one of the strands of her wavy hair got snagged on the dog's teeth.

Leo ached to talk to her, but he couldn't think of anything to say. After a few minutes, she walked to the door, said good-bye, and left. He felt like a fool and cursed his tongue-tied shyness. She must have been bored. But then he remembered the smile she had given him before she closed the door—so warm and friendly. Perhaps she liked him. Next time, if there was a next time, he would force himself to talk.

That evening, he ate for the first time in days and almost at once felt stronger. He thanked Mrs. Zohn for everything she'd done for him and started to apologize for all the work he'd given her. She hushed him.

"Stuff and nonsense, I'm just happy to see you getting well." She picked up his empty plate and went toward the door.

"Will Klara come tomorrow?" he said.

"Well, it's funny you should ask that, because she asked me if I would mind her coming. I think she must like your dog," she chuckled. For a moment, he believed her, and then she winked. "Although I suppose it could be you."

Chapter 41

HE FELT WEAK AND UNSTEADY WHEN HE GOT OUT OF BED, BUT he made himself go down the stairs to the little outhouse, where Mrs. Zohn had filled a tin bath with warm water. He soaked himself for a long time and washed his hair. Then, he dressed in the clothes Mrs. Zohn had cleaned and ironed for him. He was tired when he went back to his room, but instead of giving in to his tiredness and lying down on the bed, he sat in the armchair by the window. Bel jumped up on his lap, and he stroked her while he waited.

He was dozing when Bel stirred. She jumped off his knees and went and stood near the door, her head cocked in expectation. There was a flurry outside in the corridor, and then the door opened. Klara came in. She had tied her hair back roughly, so her cheekbones and beautiful eyes seemed more dramatic than ever. Leo instantly forgot all the words he had rehearsed in his head, but it didn't matter, because she beamed a bright smile at him and advanced into the room talking nonstop.

"You're up! Oh, good. And you look better. A bit pale and thin, but much better. Father told me you would be. But he's asked me to check you and report back to him, so poke your tongue out. That looks fine. Give me your wrist so I can take your pulse. Don't talk—I've got to count."

Leo did as she told him, and then looked in her violet eyes while she silently counted.

"Excellent. It's strong and steady," she said, letting go of his wrist. "I'll tell him you're making good progress. You're so lucky. Did you know that?"

"Why?" he asked.

"Because you were treated by my father, of course. He's the best doctor in the neighborhood, perhaps in the whole of Prussia. Do you know he's been asked to go to Berlin and Paris to give lectures at the universities there? He's written articles for medical journals, and professors write to him for advice all the time. He saved your life. How many other doctors around here know about rehydrating cholera patients? I'll tell you—not one. But he does, because he's been in correspondence with a doctor in England who pioneered the technique. So you see how lucky you are?"

Leo nodded, and he realized that he really was.

"Exactly. You are. There are hundreds dying of cholera from Warszawa down to Danzig. Father says that all people need to do is boil the water before they drink it, but do they listen? No. Some of them just don't believe in modern methods. They'd rather try to cure themselves by drinking vodka or getting some old witchy woman to cook up a ridiculous potion! You must have contracted the disease when you swallowed all that water in the river, while you were trying to rescue your friend. That must have been terrible for you."

"It was."

"How did it happen?"

He didn't want to seem like a fool again by remaining silent, so he told her the whole story. It was hard at first, but there was something about the way she listened that encouraged him to go on. When he finished, she asked questions—at first about Tomasz and Patryk, and then about his family and his village.

It became easier and easier to talk, and finally he started asking her questions.

Soon, all the barriers were down, and they were chatting and laughing like old friends.

"You haven't told me about your mother," he said.

"She's dead. She died while she was giving birth to me. Even my father couldn't save her. Look, this is her portrait," Klara said, opening a pendant that hung around her neck and showing a small photograph inside. "Isn't she beautiful? Father said she was the most beautiful woman he's ever seen, but I expect he's exaggerating. She is lovely, though."

"Yes, she is," Leo said, gazing at the woman who looked so like her daughter.

For a moment, Klara's face was sad and thoughtful. Then she clicked the pendant closed and smiled. "Come on. It's a beautiful day outside. Father said you ought to get some air and sunshine if you were up to it. And you are, aren't you?"

He couldn't resist, so they went out and walked slowly along the streets. Klara did most of the talking, and he was happy to listen and absorb her enthusiasm and energy. It was almost like having Tomasz back.

They wandered into a large park and sat on a bench in the shade of a lime tree and watched a couple of red squirrels chasing each other along the branches.

"Do you think they're playing or fighting?" Leo asked.

"Fighting, probably," she said, with a sigh. "That's all there is at the moment. War, war, war. I hate it. It's in all the newspapers, and Father and his friends talk about it all the time."

"Are we winning?"

"I suppose so. The French invaded us, but they were driven back, and they've lost three battles in three days. But there have been terrible casualties on both sides. Apparently there were ten thousand killed a few days ago at a place called Woerth. Ten thousand! All those brothers and sons dead. Our housekeeper, Rosa, says the only real winner in a war is the grave, and she's right. It's barbaric. I read in the paper that during the battle, the French released wild animals from the zoo, hoping they would kill some of our men. Lions and tigers and bears running free. Can you imagine that? And now the French soldiers are poisoning all the wells as they retreat. Unbelievable."

She shook her head and watched as one of the squirrels jumped to the ground and skittered away to another tree.

"I've met dozens of French people," she went on. "They used to visit Father all the time, and they were charming and kind and funny. But war turns countries mad. They're mad, and we're mad. You don't want to be a soldier, I hope. Good. What work do you want to do?"

"I don't know, really," Leo said, realizing that he had never really thought about it. "A farmer, perhaps."

"I want to be a doctor."

"But you're a girl."

"Don't be ridiculous. If a doctor saved your life, would you care if it was a man or a woman?"

"No," Leo admitted. "But there aren't women doctors, are there?"

"There are nurses and midwives. And Father says there have been women doctors in England and America for over ten years— only a few, but some. It can't be long before it happens here too. And when it does, I'm going to be the first. That's why he takes me out to visit patients and explains the symptoms and remedies to me afterward. I even help with his research. I watch his experiments and jot down notes for him to write up in detail later."

They walked back through the hot streets, and Leo felt exhausted by the time they got back to the rabbi's house.

"Shall we meet tomorrow?" Klara asked as they lingered in the courtyard outside the back door.

"Yes, I'd like to."

"We could go to my house. I'm sure Father would be interested to see how much you've improved. I suppose you'll want to be moving on again soon."

"I don't know," Leo said. It was another thing he hadn't thought about. How long would the rabbi let him stay? How long did he want to stay in Dirschau? Just thinking about moving on to Danzig made him feel weary. He didn't want to be alone again.

That evening, he ate downstairs with Rabbi and Mrs. Zohn, and at the end of the meal, he asked if he could stay with them a little longer.

"As long as you like," Mrs. Zohn said. "It's good to have a young person about the place again, isn't it, dear?"

The rabbi glanced at his wife for a moment, and a silent understanding passed between them. He nodded.

"I'll pay, of course. I have Tomasz's money," Leo said.

"I won't hear of it," the rabbi said. "You're a guest in our house, and a guest does not pay. Patryk already gave me more than enough for the funeral costs, so I'll not think of taking more. Besides, he told me that you come from a large family that has great need. Better you should send some of that money home to them. In the meantime, stay and be welcome."

Chapter 42

"WOULD YOU MIND IF I TOOK SOME OF YOUR BLOOD?" DR. Goldszmit asked. "It's for my research. I'd like to look at it under the microscope. I don't think much work has been done on the blood of cholera patients. It's rather exciting, don't you think? You never know what we might find. Klara and I examined some of your feces while you were in the coma. It was mostly mucus, of course—a pale, milky color, and flecked with dead cells from your intestine. Fascinating."

"Father, you're making him embarrassed," Klara said, avoiding Leo's eyes.

"Good Lord, I hope not. Never feel embarrassed by things of the body, young man. It was a real education for both of us. Anyway, what do you say about giving a little blood?" Dr. Goldszmit said, holding up a large hypodermic syringe. "Doesn't hurt much."

"If you like," Leo said. He looked away, keeping his eyes fixed on the hundreds of books lining the wall of the doctor's study while Klara tied a rubber tube around his upper arm and her father slid the needle into a vein.

"There, all done," the doctor said, holding up the syringe. "Good, deep red color. Now, Klara and I are going to have a look at this in my little laboratory. You could go to the kitchen and ask Rosa to give you some cake as a reward for this blood, or if you're interested, you could stay with us and take a look at your own blood through my microscope. I think you might find it fascinating."

Leo chose to stay, and it was fascinating. In fact, Dr. Goldszmit managed to make everything seem fascinating, and over the next few days Leo spent most of his time with him and Klara.

In the mornings, he went with them in their pony and trap, visiting patients in the town and surrounding villages. He stayed outside while they went in to see the sick people, but as they trotted on to the next call with Bel running alongside they always talked to him about what they'd found and how they were treating the illness. Leo became more and more interested, and he finally plucked up courage to start asking questions. One day, he asked why some people in a family got ill—with a cough, for example—and others didn't.

Dr. Goldszmit turned to him with a big smile and said, "Now, that's an interesting question and, frankly, one to which I have no answer. Klara's right. You really do have an inquiring mind."

In the afternoons, while Dr. Goldszmit took a nap and then read the paper or one of his medical journals, Leo and Klara sat in the garden talking or went into the kitchen and helped the house-keeper, Rosa, with the cooking. Rosa always made a big fuss over him, giving him slices of cake or letting him lick the spoon when she finished preparing a dish. She was incredibly thin herself, but she kept saying that he needed to eat more.

"You're a good-looking young chap, and you've got a sweet nature, but you need to build yourself up. Isn't that right?" she said, winking wickedly at Klara.

One afternoon, Leo sat at the Goldszmits' kitchen table and wrote a short note to his family:

"This money is for you. It is honest money. You will be able to buy chickens and geese, and Dorota can come home. Leo."

Klara and Rosa helped him wrap eight of Tomasz's heavy silver coins in paper and put them in a box filled with old bits of cloth, so they wouldn't rattle around. Leo laid the note on the top of the cloth and went to close the box.

"Wait a minute," Rosa said, pointing to the note. "You've only written 'Leo'—not a word of love!"

"Rosa!" Klara exclaimed. "It's private."

"Oh, never mind 'private.' How will his poor family feel if he just signs a cold 'Leo' at the end? Go on, boy, pick up that pen. Write, 'I love you and pray for you.' There's plenty of space. Go on. There, that's better! Right. Let's get this parcel properly wrapped now."

They covered the box with thick brown paper, tied it with string, and put some sealing wax on the knots. Leo wrote Papa's name and address on it, and he and Klara walked to the post office and sent it.

It was the first thing Leo had ever posted, and he imagined the parcel's journey back the way he had come: up the Wisła to Bromberg, then to Nakel, and finally to Wilhelmsdorf. Mail for the village was always delivered to the priest's house, and he could imagine the excitement when his family heard that there was a parcel waiting for them to collect. He pictured them rushing home with it, and then standing around while Papa opened it at the table. How would they spend the money? How much difference would it make to their lives?

When they got back from the post office, there were four men sitting in the garden talking to Dr. Goldszmit, but he signaled to Klara and Leo to come and sit next to him and listen to the conversation while Rosa served tea and cake. They were discussing the latest news about the war, and Klara soon got fidgety and went inside to help Rosa. Leo stayed. He could hardly believe that he was listening to people who had actually met King Wilhelm, Prince Friedrich Karl, and the generals who were fighting the war.

It was a world so different from the one he knew. It was a world of elegant clothes, of servants, of white hands that had never known dirty work, of cigars and the smell of perfume, of fine coaches waiting outside, of the time to discuss politics and read newspapers, and of discovery and exciting ideas. It was a world that entranced him. Perhaps if he stayed here, got work here—helping Dr. Goldszmit?—perhaps it was a world he could share.

Afterward, Dr. Goldszmit took him into his study and unrolled a map and showed him the places that the men had talked about—Saarbrucken and Wissembourg and Metz.

"History is being made here," the doctor said, tapping the map. "For good or for ill, I'm not sure which. The one thing I do know is that with over a million Prussian soldiers mobilized and ready to fight, there will be much blood spilled."

He stared at the map, lost in thought, and then shook his head and sighed.

"All that pain and suffering. It's all human madness, of course, but what to do, Leo? That's the problem—what to do."

That night, Leo found it hard to sleep. His head was filled with the things he had heard discussed—battles and weapons and tactics. He pictured Prussia's three armies racing across the border into France. He saw soldiers shooting and bayoneting. He could hear the boom of the Krupp six-pounder cannons from the Prussian side and the rattle of the French mitrailleuse, spitting out seventy-five bullets a minute, on the other.

And then there was the waking dream that had invaded his mind, a dream he had told himself was impossible but that just wouldn't go away. Rabbi Zohn and his wife seemed happy to let him stay, and he enjoyed the calm, gentle time he spent with them in the evenings. So perhaps it was possible, his dream. Perhaps he could live here in Dirschau and become part of the world of Klara and Dr. Goldszmit.

Chapter 43

Dr. Goldszmit was not his usual talkative self as they made the rounds of his patients. There was a frown on his face, and he seemed distracted and distant, barely responding when Leo asked him questions.

"Is something wrong?" Leo whispered to Klara after one visit. But at that moment, her father came out of the house and she quickly shook her head and put her finger to her lips. A sudden fear ran through Leo. Was the doctor displeased with him? This was such a new world for him. It would be easy to do or say something wrong without realizing.

The rest of the morning was agony as they went from house to house with only the sound of the pony's hoofbeats and the creak of the turning wheels to break the silence. When they finally trotted back into their courtyard, Leo offered to unhitch the pony. Dr. Goldszmit accepted with a nod of his head and a brief smile that was gone even before he turned away toward the back door.

Leo undid the traces and then led the pony into its stable. He poured water into its drinking trough and was rubbing down the pony's sweating flanks when Klara came in.

"What's the matter?" he asked, going to her at once.

"It's the war," she said, and a huge feeling of relief swept through him. "There's been another battle—the biggest yet, at a place called Mars-La-Tour."

"Did we lose?"

"No, we won, but at a terrible cost. Over fifteen thousand of our soldiers were killed or injured. Heaven knows what the casualties are on the French side. Father's upset about it, I know he is. And I can see he's thinking about it all the time, but he won't say anything. I'm worried about him."

"Don't be," Leo said, taking her hand and squeezing it. "He'll soon start talking again. You know what a talker he is."

She chuckled. "Yes, he is. Thank you." She raised his hand to her lips and kissed it.

There was a moment of stillness as he looked into her violet-blue eyes and his heart swelled. Then she made a funny face and let his hand drop, as if it had been a joke. But he knew it hadn't been.

Early that evening, Rabbi Zohn took Leo to a stonemason and they chose a headstone for Tomasz's grave.

"Just Tomasz—no family name?" the stonemason asked.

"I don't know it," Leo said.

"Tomasz it is, then. Nothing else?"

Leo thought. "Yes, you can write, 'A Good Friend.'"

Rabbi Zohn nodded in approval.

"Nice and simple—they're the best," the stonemason said. "Be ready the day after tomorrow."

The mound of earth over Tomasz's grave had settled when Leo and the rabbi went out to the cemetery two days later to watch the headstone being put into place.

"Perfect," the stonemason said, standing back to admire his handiwork. "'A Good Friend.' Let's hope people say that about us when it comes our turn, eh?"

Mrs. Zohn had picked some flowers for both of them, and Leo laid his on top of Tomasz's grave. He expected the rabbi to do the same, but instead, he turned away and walked to the far side of the cemetery. Leo quickly paid the stonemason for the work and went over to the rabbi, who was laying the flowers on another grave.

"What does it say?" Leo asked, pointing to the Hebrew inscription on the gravestone.

Without looking at the words, the rabbi recited, "Here are buried Rebekah and Lea, of blessed memory. Our eyes are blinded by sorrow."

"Who were they?"

"Our daughters," Rabbi Zohn said, bending down and plucking some weeds. He gently patted the ground. "There was an epidemic of scarlet fever fifteen years ago, and we lost them both. Rebekah first. She was only six, and full of smiles and energy and laughter. All gone. Then four days later, my Lea too. It was...unbearable. She was your age. Lovely. And sweet and kind."

The rabbi stood up and sighed deeply.

"My wife was like a lion when you were ill, so determined that you would live. She couldn't abide the loss of another child in our house." He turned and smiled. "Especially with the name Leo—so like our Lea. You should have heard her prayers—'Keep him safe. Keep him safe.' She spoke so fiercely that the Lord must have been afraid to deny her!"

Leo suddenly thought of the note the soldier, Konrad, had given him—"Stay safe." Was Konrad still safe, or was he among all those dead and wounded in France? "Stay safe." He had been in danger of dying of cholera but Dr. Goldszmit and Mrs. Zohn had kept him alive, so perhaps Konrad had survived too.

Church bells were ringing as they made their way back into town, and the main square was thronging with crowds.

"What's happening?" Leo asked one of the passersby.

"A victory for our army at Gravelotte. The French are on the run!" the man shouted above the din.

Leo could hardly contain his impatience as he accompanied Rabbi Zohn back to the synagogue. Then he ran to Dr. Goldszmit's house, wondering if the news had reached them. From a distance, he could see Klara sitting alone on the veranda steps. He waved, but she didn't wave back.

"There's been another battle," he called, opening the gate and running toward her.

She nodded and looked down at the ground.

"Why so sad?" he asked. "It's a victory! The French are on the run."

She lifted her beautiful eyes to him, and tears were brimming on her lashes.

"Father is going to France. That's what he's been worrying about these past days—where is he needed most, here or there? Then last night, he got a telegram from a general he knows, saying that hundreds of soldiers are dying for lack of doctors. So he made up his mind. He's leaving tomorrow."

"But who will look after you?" Leo asked, and for an instant, he pictured her coming to live with him at Rabbi Zohn's house. Then he said, "Rosa, I suppose."

Klara shook her head, wiped the tears from her eyes, and sat up straighter.

"I'm going with him, Leo."

"But…you can't."

"Father needs me. I can look after him. I can help him. And think what an experience it will be for me. I want to be a doctor, Leo. It's my destiny. I want it more than anything."

She looked straight at him and urged him to understand exactly what she meant. There were no tears in her eyes now—only determination, and he knew that nothing would change her mind.

Chapter 44

Dr. Goldszmit and Klara had been given seats on a military train, and Dirschau station echoed with the stamp of soldiers' boots and the blare of a brass band playing stirring marches. The platform was crowded with embracing couples, crying children, and parents bidding farewell to their sons. As Leo weaved his way among them, he tried not to think about the approaching moment when, like these people, he would have to say good-bye to someone he loved.

They reached the front carriage, and Dr. Goldszmit stood back and let his daughter organize the loading of their luggage onto the train. Leo watched her calmly giving instructions to the porter and realized that she was right, the doctor did need her to help him. He depended on her.

She turned, now, and came toward them smiling and looking so much older than her fourteen years—a young woman in her neat brown jacket and long checked skirt. And yes, he could see that she would be afraid of nothing at the battlefront—the blood, the cries of wounded men, the amputations, and the death. She would stand beside her father and help him, and all the time she would be learning, so one day she would realize her destiny and become a doctor.

Seeing her like this—so confident and capable, so grown up—he could hardly believe the foolish dreams he had carried in his heart. During their two brief weeks of friendship and laughter together, the age difference between them had seemed nothing, but now it felt enormous. She was a young woman, and he was like a child, lost and directionless.

"I think we'll have to board, Father," she said, glancing up at the big clock.

Leo followed her gaze and saw a pigeon land on top of the clock and peer down at the chaos below.

"Yes, yes," Dr. Goldszmit said. "Well, Leo…"

He held out his hand, and Leo shook it.

"What are your plans? Will you be staying in Dirschau?"

The question took Leo by surprise, but he knew the answer at once. He shook his head. No, he would not stay.

The doctor nodded, and then put one hand on his daughter's shoulder and the other on Leo's. "We all have our own paths, and we have to follow them. But perhaps our paths will cross again one day. Let us hope so."

There was a whistle blast, and carriage doors began to slam shut all the way down the train.

"We have to go, Father," Klara said.

Dr. Goldszmit patted the top of Leo's head and climbed the steps onto the train.

And now there was just Klara in front of him. Then she came close and her lips brushed his cheek.

"Say you understand," she whispered.

"I do," he said.

She stepped back, and those extraordinary violet eyes gazed at him intently, as if she was fixing his image inside her brain.

"We have become such good friends. I will miss you," she said.

"I'll miss you."

"Wherever you go, let me know. Write and let me know. Promise me."

He nodded.

"You'll have a good life," she said. "And we will meet again one day. We will."

Her voice cracked, and she turned away quickly and walked toward the train. Then she stopped and came back.

"I don't know anything about love," she said, and she looked at him as if she was puzzled and amused at the same time.

Leo didn't know what to say. There was another whistle blast, and Klara glanced down the platform.

"We're going," she said, almost to herself. Then she spoke directly to him. "I don't know if it is love, but my heart is full of you."

He wanted to say, "Yes, yes—that is what I feel too," but he just stood there.

"I have never kissed a boy," she said. "Not properly. I want you to be the first, so I will never forget."

She put her hands on either side of his face, and he closed his eyes. He felt her lips press against his. They stayed there for long seconds, and then she pulled his face even closer. Her mouth opened slightly, and her breath mixed with his. Her tongue ran across his lips, and he shivered with delight.

Then it was over.

She let go of him and hurried back to the train. She mounted the three steps into the carriage. She didn't look back as she closed the door.

He began to walk. Down the platform, not turning around. Hurrying his way among all those waving, weeping people while steam hissed and the train began to clank and chug its way out of the station.

Chapter 45

I GUESSED IT," RABBI ZOHN SAID WHEN LEO TOLD HIM THAT HE was leaving. "I saw it in your eyes yesterday when you came back from the station—there's nothing to keep you here now. But I hope you won't forget us."

"How could I forget someone who saved my life?" Leo said, looking at Mrs. Zohn.

"That was the good doctor, not me," she said, blushing and smiling shyly.

She insisted on quickly wrapping a parcel of food to take with him, and the rabbi put it in a small canvas knapsack. Mrs. Zohn hugged him.

"Take care, child, and write when you can—there are people here who will be praying for you."

Outside in the courtyard, he offered one of the silver coins to the rabbi. "Can you give it to the gravedigger and ask him to tend Tomasz's grave for me?"

"That's a good thought. I shall ensure that it's done."

Leo held out his hand, but the rabbi took him by the shoulders and embraced him briefly. "Go well with the Lord."

Bel seemed to guess that they were leaving, and she ran ahead and turned toward the river. He whistled her back, because he felt he had to pay one last visit to Tomasz. He wanted to ask his advice about what to do, and where to go. But even as he walked toward the cemetery, it was as if he could already hear Tomasz's voice urging him: "America. Go to America!"

He stood by the graveside with Bel next to him and spoke his silent thoughts, but he realized he could have spoken them anywhere. He wasn't closer to Tomasz here at his grave. He didn't feel his presence more keenly.

Tomasz was with him everywhere now, part of his thoughts and his being.

He closed the cemetery gate and followed Bel as she raced ahead of him, down to the river and out toward the edge of town.

For the first time in a long time, he was on his own again, and all his senses were alert and wary. People were moving at a faster pace than usual, keeping their eyes down as he passed them, and there was an air of tension and dread. A woman sat on the front step of her cottage, weeping and sobbing, while her four young children stood and stared at her in confusion.

A young man thundered past him on a horse, almost forcing him off the track, and a few minutes later, two other men galloped past in pursuit.

As the sun sank behind the line of low hills miles away across the plain, he knocked at the door of a house at a crossroads to ask permission to sleep in the barn. There was a long pause, and then he knocked again.

"I've told you before. My son's not here," came the voice of an old woman. "He's gone to the war."

"I would like to rest the night in your barn," Leo called. "I can pay."

"He's not here. I've got a gun," quavered the woman's voice.

"I only want—" Leo began, but the door shook as the old woman hit it from the inside.

He decided to move on and ended up spending the night under a willow tree farther down the road. He remembered the old saying that willow trees sucked the soul out of people who slept beneath them, but there were no other trees, and he needed shelter from the drizzle that had started to fall. The ground felt hard after his weeks in a soft bed, and he passed a long, uncomfortable night with only brief, fitful moments of sleep.

During the next three days, Leo and Bel made their way across a low, wet countryside, a land of ponds and lagoons and boggy soil that sucked at their feet. They often had to jump ditches or little rivulets, and sometimes the wider streams forced them to make long detours in order to find a bridge. Everywhere, there was the trickle or rush of water flowing toward the main river. The few occupied houses they saw were perched on little knolls of higher ground. Those on lower ground were mostly empty and crumbling, and bore waterlines on their walls as proof of how often they had been flooded. Gulls circled overhead, crying forlornly, and ducks burst into the air with frantic, flapping wings. The only people they saw were fishermen and the occasional traveler heading toward one of the ferries that crossed the sluggish river.

Then, toward the end of the third day, there was a new smell in the air—an odor Leo couldn't place. They were walking along a straight stretch of river when, up ahead, he could see that it broadened considerably. Beyond that was the sparkle of a wider stretch of water. His heart began to beat faster. Could it be? He started to run.

The land rose, and he found himself climbing up a sand dune through a pine wood. He was panting when he reached the crest, but he scampered down the other side, through the trees, with Bel racing ahead of him excitedly until, suddenly, they burst out of the wood and found themselves on a wide beach of golden sand.

And there, smelling wild and salty, and dancing with silver-speckled waves, was the sea.

He had often tried to picture what it would look like, but he had never been able to imagine anything so immense. Leo was overwhelmed by the sight. He fell to his knees and gazed and gazed.

He had made it.

Chapter 46

I T TOOK ANOTHER TWO DAYS TO MAKE HIS WAY ALONG THE coast to Danzig. At night, he slept in the dunes, soothed by the rhythm of the breaking waves and warmed by the closeness of Bel. During the daytime, on the long, tiring slog along the beach, he gazed in awe at the ceaseless movement of the sea, watching how the immense stretch of water changed color endlessly with the mood of the sky—from blue to gray, and from golden to bloody in the light of the rising or setting sun.

Then, quite suddenly, the houses began, and, after days of peace and harmony, he walked into a wild town of noise and movement. The closer he got to the center of Danzig, the more violent and mad the people seemed. Men reeled from one tavern to the next, accompanied by women who screeched with laughter.

Ahead of him, a fight suddenly broke out, and two men fell sprawling into the gutter, scattering some pigs that were rooting through the rubbish. The men got up again and hurled themselves at each other with shouts and curses. There was a flurry of flying fists, and then it all stopped as quickly as it had begun. A few moments later, the fighters staggered away arm in arm, singing like old friends.

A gang of shrieking urchins came running out of one of the narrow side lanes, dodging in and out of the passersby who all stood back as if afraid. The leader skidded to a halt near Leo and held up his hand to stop his followers. They were younger and smaller than Leo—some of them no more than about seven or eight years old—but there were nearly a dozen of them, and he knew he wouldn't stand much of a chance if they attacked.

They stared at him, their greedy eyes trying to decide if he was worth robbing, and he prayed that his belt with the precious coins was well hidden under his waistcoat. He grasped his stick more tightly, ready to defend himself, but the leader looked him over, spat on the ground, and then darted away down an alleyway, followed by his gang.

Farther along the road, three dogs were lying next to a fence, but they sprang to their feet when they saw Bel. They barked and snarled, baring their fangs as if they had been infected by the madness in the air. Bel stopped, the hackles raised along her back. She looked ready to stand her ground and fight, but Leo called her away and headed down the nearest side street.

They came out onto a road packed with people all moving in the same direction. They were caught up with the crowd as it shuffled forward and then funneled through an arched gateway and across a bridge. These people weren't rowdy and wild like the others he'd seen in town—on the contrary, hardly anyone spoke—but hemmed in among them, Leo felt uneasy. Where were they going? Their faces were grim, their eyes were fixed and intense, and they seemed gripped by a suppressed excitement.

Now they were heading uphill, filing along a path between high banks—around one bend, and then another. The pace of the crowd slowed as the slope became steeper, and a kind of impatient tension shivered through the people, as if they were worried they would be late for something. The gap between the banks narrowed, pressing everyone closer, and Leo reached down and grabbed Bel by the scruff of her neck, worried that she might be trampled underfoot. Then, suddenly, the path came out onto wide level ground and the crowd surged forward in all directions.

Leo found himself standing on a high hill. Away to the left, he could see the rooftops and spires of Danzig and, in between the buildings, glimpses of sunlight flashing on water. In front of him, the hill sloped down toward a large fort, where the black-and-white Prussian flag fluttered from a flagpole on top of the main gate. All the people were looking for a vantage point on the slope and, without knowing why, he moved forward and joined them.

He found a place that had a clear view of the fort, and he watched as columns of soldiers marched out from behind one of the buildings and began to form lines on three sides of a square. The crowd on the hill was hushed, and every stamp of the soldiers' boots and every shouted command from their officer rose up clearly from below.

"Attention!" he ordered, and the soldiers obeyed.

There was a moment's silence, and then six more soldiers marched out from behind the barracks. They were carrying rifles, and a murmur ran through the crowd at the sight of them.

"What's going on?" Leo whispered to a man standing next to him.

"That's the firing squad," the man said.

"What for?" Leo asked, a feeling of dread filling his chest.

"They're shooting a young lad for desertion—a Polish lad, a patriot through and through. He refused to fight their damned Prussian war, and they're going to execute him for it."

"Detail halt!" the officer ordered from below, and the six soldiers came to a stop. "Right turn." The soldiers turned.

Now Leo saw what he hadn't noticed before. The soldiers had

turned and were facing a stake that had been driven into the ground in front of a wall.

An instant later, the crowd stirred as a door opened in one of the buildings. A young man in a white shirt and black trousers was led out by two soldiers, each of them gripping him by his elbows. Behind them came a priest in a purple robe. The man was led to the post and he stood calmly, unresisting, while the two soldiers shackled his legs to the base. They pulled his arms roughly behind him and fastened his hands at the back.

The silence was total, and Leo could hear his blood beating in his ear.

The priest leaned toward the young man and began reading from the prayer book in his hand. When he finished, the priest raised his hand and made the sign of the cross, and then he stood back as the officer stepped forward and wrapped a blindfold around the man's eyes. Then he pulled something out of his pocket and pinned it to the upper left side of the man's shirt. It was a red cut-out of a heart. The target.

The officer marched back to the side of the firing squad and then spun around on his heels, clicking his boots to attention. He drew his saber from its hilt and glanced up to the sky, his head cocked.

"He's waiting for noon," the man next to Leo whispered.

The silence was dreadful, and Leo's face burned with the tension and horror of the wait. What was the man feeling? Tied and blindfolded, waiting through his final seconds before death? What must he be thinking? How could he endure it?

A cold wind blew across the hill and, down below, it caught the loose folds of the man's shirt, making it billow back and forth so the cut-out heart seemed to throb and tremble like his real heart inside.

Then came a voice. A single, shaky, voice singing.

"While we live, she is existing…"

It was the first line of Dabrowski's "Mazurka"—the banned Polish anthem.

Who had sung it?

It came again, stronger now, and everyone saw who the singer was—the young man tied to that stake.

"While we live, she is existing…"

He was inviting the crowd to join in. He began the "Mazurka" again, and this time, hundreds of voices joined him from the hill.

"While we live, she is existing
Poland is not fallen
We will win, with swords resisting
What the foe has stolen."

Below, a few of the soldiers glanced up nervously at the masses on the hill. The officer shifted his feet, uncertain of what to do.

Then a bell boomed the first note of noon and the officer raised his saber. The singing was too loud to hear his commands, but Leo could see his mouth move. The six soldiers raised their rifles, took one step forward, and aimed.

The "Mazurka" reached its last note, and the singing stopped just as the officer ordered, "Fire!"

The volley of shots rattled in the square. The man jerked backward and then slumped down. A couple of seconds later, the whole of his shirt front flooded with blood, and the cut-out heart was lost in the wide red stain.

Bel whimpered, and Leo could stand no more. He whirled around and pushed his way through the people who were all rooted to the spot, staring, fascinated by the death below.

He reached the back of the crowd and ran down the hill, across the bridge, through the archway, and back into the warren of streets. He stopped to catch his breath and felt his legs trembling, his knees almost giving way. He took a few steps and then collapsed onto the step of the doorway as a terrible weakness seized him. Bel looked at him with her beautiful brown eyes and nuzzled his hand, begging him to stroke her. He pulled her toward him and buried his face in the soft warmth of the fur around her neck, holding her tight and trying to drive away the horror of the execution.

A few minutes later, Bel started to growl, and Leo raised his head. A man was standing in the road, looking at him. He had very short black hair, and his square face was tanned to a nut brown color.

"What's the matter with your dog?" the man said. "I was only going to ask if you were all right, and she's baring her fangs like a crazy wolf."

"Ssh, Bel," Leo said, pulling her and making her sit.

"Were you up there?" the man asked, gesturing toward the hill. "I thought so. You look as pale as a ghost. Killing our own soldiers, eh? It's a mad world. They'll start on us sailors next."

"Are you in the navy?"

"The fighting navy? No, I've got too much sense for that. Merchant ships, that's me. And they won't shoot us, because they need us for trade. Not that there's much trade at the moment."

"Why?"

"The French navy is blockading the Baltic Sea, isn't it? No ships have gone anywhere for the last month. But now that their army's surrendered, I reckon we'll be back at sea in a couple of days."

"We've beaten the French?" Leo asked, immediately thinking of Klara and Dr. Goldszmit.

"Crushed them. Their whole army has been taken prisoner— old Napoleon the Third, his generals, the lot," the man said, and then looked along the road toward the sound of voices and footsteps. "They're all coming back from the execution. It'll be a madhouse here. I'm moving on down to the docks. You coming? The name's Casimir."

"Leo," he said, shaking the man's hand. "And this is Bel."

Bel growled again as Casimir bent to stroke her, but he laughed and patted her anyway. "She'll get used to me. Dogs always love me," he said as they began walking. "I had two dogs when I was a kid. Beautiful, they were. Followed me everywhere."

But Leo wasn't really listening. He couldn't help thinking about what Casimir had said: no ships had left port for a month. Perhaps Patryk hadn't been able sell his timber yet, and perhaps he was still here in Danzig. How good it would be to find a friend in this violent, frightening town.

Chapter 47

THE AREA AROUND THE DOCKS WAS EVEN ROWDIER THAN THE rest of town. Taverns were overflowing, and drunken sailors staggered along the docksides or sat slumped on the pavement.

"You can't blame them. It's this damned blockade," Casimir said. "Us seafarers hate being stranded on dry land. What else is there to do but get drunk with your shipmates? And it was worse a month ago when everyone was flush with money, but now pockets are getting empty. The fights are getting worse, though! Every day, a couple of lads end up with someone's knife stuck in their guts. You'll have to keep your wits about you. I'm warning you."

Casimir acted as Leo's guide through the docks, under the cranes, and past all the idle ships, including his own, a fine four-masted clipper called the *Marsalla*. They tramped across bridges, up creeks, and along the quays of the canals and rivers, with Leo checking every face they passed. But there was no sign of Patryk.

"I reckon this fellow left his raft with an agent and is on his way back upriver to get his next cargo," Casimir finally said as night began to fall. "Where are you sleeping tonight?"

Leo shrugged.

"Can't ask you back to my lodgings. There's six of us in a bed as it is!" Casimir laughed. "Perhaps I'll meet up with you tomorrow. I'll probably be at the Bread-Seller's Gate or around Mariacka Street in the afternoon. Take care."

Leo wandered through the town, looking for somewhere to pass the night. He thought of going back to the hilltop but decided he'd only have nightmares about the execution. In the end, he settled down in the porch of a church. A statue of the Virgin Mary looked down at him and, with Bel snuggled up close for warmth, he managed to sleep until dawn.

He got up and went across to the fountain in front of the church. As he splashed the cold water on his face, he realized that he was just wasting time looking for Patryk. The really important task was to find a ship to America. He bought some bread and sausage and shared it with Bel as they walked back toward the docks. Perhaps this blockade was a piece of luck for him—all these ships were waiting, and there were probably dozens of them bound for America. And they'd all be putting to sea in the next couple of days, so he was sure to find one that would take him.

He walked along the docks, stopping at each ship to ask someone on board where they were going.

"Nowhere, till the Frenchies let us!" was the usual joke before the sailor gave the real destination.

Finland, Sweden, Norway, Scotland, England, Portugal, Spain—not one was bound for America. Most of the sailors gave him a brief reply and then told him to move on, but on one ship, an older sailor invited him to sit and talk. He had short gray hair, and his deeply lined face, tanned by wind and sun, reminded Leo of all the farmers he had ever known.

"America? Well, if you're looking for a passenger ship, lad, you'll be best off going to Stettin or Hamburg."

"I don't want a passenger ship. I want to work," Leo said. "My friend told me that ships are always looking for sailors, and they let you work instead of paying your fare."

"Did he now?" the old man chuckled. "Well, that would soon put us old tars out of work, wouldn't it? I think your friend got his facts a bit wrong. Oh, I dare say it happens from time to time, but now, with the whole port heaving with sailors aching to get back to sea? I don't think so. No, your best idea is to go to Stettin or Hamburg. It's quite a journey—Stettin's a couple of hundred kilometers, and Hamburg's double that or more—but I tell you, your chances of getting work on a ship from here are very slim."

Casimir said the same thing when they met up in the afternoon.

"Too many experienced sailors around, Leo. Who's going to want a novice like you?"

"I don't want to be paid. I'll work for nothing if I can go to America."

"Yes, and so will hundreds of others. Come on. Don't look downhearted. You ever tried hot chocolate? No? Well, I'll buy you one to cheer you up."

Casimir was in high spirits because the news was sweeping the port that the French fleet had started to lift the blockade. He'd been to his ship, the *Marsalla*, and the captain had told him they would be sailing the next day. He'd even advanced him some cash against his pay.

"It's not a lot, but I don't want the money to get seasick, so I'd better spend it before I get on board!"

They went into the nearest café and Casimir ordered a large vodka for himself and a hot chocolate for Leo.

"It's the best thing I've ever tasted in my life," Leo said after a couple of sips.

"Not as good as this," Casimir laughed, knocking back his glass of vodka and calling for another.

Leo drank the chocolate slowly, wanting to make the pleasure last, but he shared a bit with Bel, dipping his finger in it and letting her lick it off.

"Do you think I could get work on a passenger ship if I went to Stettin or Hamburg?" he asked Casimir when he had finally drained the last of the chocolate.

"America, America—everyone wants to go to America, Leo! There are waiting lists for paying passengers, so they're not going to let someone go for free, are they?" Casimir said, twirling his empty glass on the table. He looked up as some men at a nearby table roared with laughter. A big smile lit up his face. "Hey, there's one of my shipmates. Wait here. He owes me a drink, and there's no time like the present."

Casimir went over to the other table and sat down, joining in the laughter and calling the waitress for another vodka. Leo gazed out of the window at all the sailors making their way back to their ships, and he suddenly made up his mind. What was the point of keeping the money to start a new life in America if he couldn't even get there? Better to spend the money for the voyage, and then work to earn some more once he was there. Even Tomasz would agree if he were here.

As soon as he had made the decision, he felt all his worries lift away. He sat back, hardly able to stop smiling.

"Well, you look happier. I told you the chocolate would cheer you up," Casimir said when he got back from talking to his friends. "Come on, it's getting stuffy in here. Let's go and sniff some salty air."

They walked for a long time along the quays past the ware-houses and granaries, to where the Motlaw River joined the Wisła and widened out into a broad channel. They sat on the bank and watched the ships already making their way toward the sea.

"That'll be me tomorrow," Casimir said.

"And me, soon," Leo said. "I've made up my mind. I'm going to catch a passenger ship from Stettin or Hamburg."

"Leo, I've already told you—"

"I'll pay," Leo broke in. Then he added in a low voice, "I've got money."

"Oh, yes? How much? Two pfennigs?" Casimir mocked.

"I'm not sure how much, but a lot."

Leo glanced around. There was nobody in sight. He slipped off Tomasz's belt and shook the coins out onto the ground.

Casimir whistled in surprise when the last coin clinked down onto the pile of others. They lay there with the red of the sinking sun shining on the silver. Casimir picked a coin up and looked at it, turning it over and reading the inscription around the edge. He placed it in his mouth and bit.

"How much do you think they're worth?" Leo asked. "Enough to pay the fare?"

Casimir nodded his head slowly. "Enough for a train to Hamburg, enough for the ship, and then some left over."

Now Casimir looked around quickly.

"Put it away—before anyone notices. My God, Leo, if certain people saw this, they'd slit your throat in double quick time, believe me."

Night was beginning to fall, and Leo suddenly felt rather nervous as they walked back into the bustling town. It seemed as if almost every other passerby glanced at the belt around his waist, so he was very glad when Casimir suggested that he could spend the night in his lodgings.

"The old bat who runs the place won't notice, and a couple of the lads have already gone back to their ships. It's not luxurious, but you'll be safer there than on the street."

Chapter 48

CASIMIR'S ROOM SMELLED TERRIBLE, AND ALL FOUR OF THE MEN snored, but Leo was happy enough lying on the floor with Bel next to him. It was good to be indoors, warm and safe from robbery.

While Casimir was packing his kit bag the next morning, Leo chatted with the other sailors, asking them what they knew about ships from Stettin and Hamburg to America. One of them was certain that there were more ships from Stettin, but another said there were more from Hamburg. They were still arguing when Casimir and Leo left the room, tiptoed down the stairs past the landlady's door, and out onto the street.

"I owe her two weeks' rent, but the old bat charges too much," Casimir laughed.

They stopped at the same café, and Casimir bought another hot chocolate for Leo and a vodka for himself.

"Na Zrowie!" Casimir toasted. "Here's to your journey to the United States of America." He gulped his vodka and stood up. "Well, my young friend, I'll leave you with your hot chocolate. You take care of yourself."

He ruffled Leo's hair, patted Bel on her head, swung his kit bag over his shoulder, and headed for the door. He turned and winked, and then he was gone.

Leo sipped his hot chocolate and felt a great sadness steal over him. For months now, all he had done was meet people, get to know them, and say good-bye. There were hopes and promises that they would see each other again—Patryk, Klara, Dr. Goldszmit, Rabbi and Mrs. Zohn—but deep down, he couldn't be sure that it would ever happen.

He was still brooding about this ten minutes later, when there was a call from the door. He looked up and felt his heart lift with pleasure at seeing Casimir's beaming face again.

"Great news," Casimir said, sitting down at the table. "I can't believe the luck. I got to the end of the street and bumped into one of the best captains I've ever sailed under. He's a bit of a rogue, but a real diamond. I asked him where he was off to, and guess what? He's sailing for New York today. I couldn't believe it. Well, of course I told him about you. He said he was all crewed up already and hadn't got room for passengers, but I told him that you'd probably be willing to work and pay him a little extra too. So, as a personal favor to me, he's come up with a plan. He's going to pay off one of the young lads on board and take you in his place."

"Really?" Leo said, his heart pounding fast.

"Really! Of course, you'll have to give him the money first, so he can pay the other lad off. And he'll want a bit himself for doing you a favor—you know how things are. But it'll still work out a damn sight less than paying your fare on a passenger ship." Casimir looked around the café and lowered his voice. "Slip your belt off, and I'll go and get it all sorted."

"I'll come with you," Leo whispered back.

"No, best you stay here. I kind of exaggerated your age and size a bit, so he thinks he's getting a strapping, brawny lad of sixteen to replace the other one. Don't want him to see you and change his mind. But he's sailing in an hour, so once the other lad's gone ashore, it'll be too late to find anyone else, and he won't have much choice. Anyway, you're strong and a hard worker, aren't you? Well? Make up your mind. He won't wait forever."

Leo unwound the belt and handed it over.

"Right, give me twenty, thirty minutes to get it all set up. I'll come back to fetch you and get you safely on board."

Casimir smiled broadly as he tapped Leo's cheek.

"Your lucky day," he said, and then headed for the door.

Leo watched him go out the door and away down the street.

After fifteen minutes, Leo's face began to burn as the first stabs of suspicion entered his chest. He tried to drive the doubts away. Casimir wouldn't cheat him. He was a kind man—a friend. He had given him advice. Bought him hot chocolate. He had been nice to Bel.

Yes, but Bel didn't like him. She slunk away each time he tried to pat her. But that didn't mean anything. Dogs could be funny sometimes.

No, ever since he had left home he had only met kind people who had helped him. That wasn't going to change now. Look how Casimir had let him stay the night in his room.

Yes, but he had cheated his landlady. He had left the house without paying two weeks' rent. That was like stealing. And if he stole once, he could easily steal again.

Surely, no one would be so cruel.

What about the cart driver? He had been ready to kill Tomasz to get those silver coins. Money made people do terrible things.

The doubts grew and grew into a certainty. He knew the truth, but he wouldn't allow himself to believe it, even when twenty minutes had passed. Then twenty-five, and thirty. He sat there, cursing his stupidity and praying that it was all a mistake—praying that Casimir would come through that door at any moment.

But he didn't come.

After forty minutes, Leo jumped up from the table and burst through the door onto the street. He could hardly breathe, and his legs were trembling, but he forced himself to run—down the street to the docks, along the quayside, to where Casimir's boat had been moored.

"The *Marsalla*?" a sailor replied when Leo asked him. "She hauled anchor about half an hour ago."

Even then, he wouldn't believe it. He ran. Ran along the quay, taking the route he'd taken with Casimir the night before—out to where the Motlaw River flowed into the Wisła, hoping all the time that he would catch up with the *Marsalla*, that Casimir would see him, take pity on him, and throw the belt ashore.

When he got to the end of the quay and finally sank down onto his knees, exhausted and with all hope gone, he began to cry—not for himself, but for the end of Tomasz's dream.

Chapter 49

THE NEXT TWO DAYS PASSED IN A DAZE. HE FELT AS IF HE HAD lost everything that mattered. He didn't care if he lived or died. He looked at the world through bitter eyes and saw only ugliness and betrayal.

Then early on the third morning, as the first light of day began to break, he opened his eyes and looked out from the church porch where he had spent the night. At the base of the statue of the Virgin Mary, a pigeon was already at work, scratching around for food, strutting here and there, ducking its head to peck at something on the ground, and then moving on. The first ray of the sun hit the top of a high roof across the square and the pigeon suddenly took flight, rising almost vertically and heading for the light. It flashed across the sun's rays and disappeared behind the ridge of the roof.

Leo sat up and realized that he had a choice. He could stay here in Danzig, scratching for enough food to keep himself alive, or he could move on. If he moved on, he had two choices. He could retrace his steps and go home to face jail, or go back and see his family evicted from their farm. Or…

Or he could go on. Go on, and do what he and Tomasz had set out to do.

Would Tomasz have given up if someone had stolen the money? No. Never. Bad things never stopped Tom. He would have cursed, and then he would have smiled and joked and carried on. That's what he always did.

It would be harder now, without the money, but he couldn't let that beat him.

And, in a way, he was free now. He had been bewildered by that money. It was money he had never liked, ever since Tomasz had nearly died on the train rather than spend it, and ever since it had weighed Tomasz down and dragged him under the water. Now it was Casimir's money, to bring him whatever it brought him—happiness or tragedy.

It was gone, and he was free to choose. Home? Or that dream?

There was no choice, really. He had to make the dream come true—for himself, for his family, and for Tomasz.

He went down to the docks again, certain that he would find a ship.

The morning passed.

The afternoon passed.

His feet ached with walking.

But still, he believed it would happen.

The evening started to draw in, and boats, heading for the open sea, glided past on the running tide, their lamps shining.

And then suddenly, he saw a long, sleek, three-masted ship. She was tied up at the dock but her small smokestack was fuming, so she was ready to depart. A man was talking to the captain of the ship at the bottom of the gangplank. As he was passing them, Leo caught the word "America."

He stopped and waited a short distance away.

Eventually, the man saluted the captain and hurried toward a brightly lit office in a warehouse. The captain took a long draw on his cigar, as though relishing his last moments on the land. Then he flipped the stub into the air and watched as it sparked and whirled down into the water. He straightened his shoulders and started up the gangplank.

"Sir," Leo called.

The captain stopped and turned.

"Do you need any hands?" Leo asked.

"No," the captain said gruffly. Then he added, more kindly, "Thank you," before continuing up the gangplank.

The kind tone gave Leo the nerve to ask again. "A cabin boy?"

The captain hesitated, turned, and came back down to the quayside. "Let me look at you."

Leo stepped forward into the light spilling from onboard. He looked up into the captain's eyes, which were assessing him keenly.

The captain nodded. "I'll take you."

"Are you going to America?"

"That's right. Copenhagen. Santander. Lisbon. Then across the wide Atlantic to America. Sailing into New York Harbor. You like the sound of that?"

All the other names meant nothing to Leo, but he nodded, accepting.

"Then come on board, young cabin boy. What's your name?"

"Leo," he said, then added, "Sir."

"Come aboard, Leo," the captain said and started back up the gangplank.

"Come on, Bel," Leo called.

The captain stopped and looked back. "Is that your dog?"

"Yes, sir."

"I'm sorry—no dogs."

Leo stepped back onto the quay. "I can't leave Bel, sir."

"No dogs," the captain repeated.

"Sir, she's come with me everywhere."

The captain shrugged and turned back, climbing up toward the ship. He stepped onto the deck and said something inaudible.

"Sir?" Leo called.

The captain looked down and beckoned. "I said, 'I'll make an exception.' I hope she's a good rat-catcher."

"Thank you, sir," Leo said, feeling relief flood through him. "Come on, Bel."

But Bel stood where she was.

"Come on, girl," Leo said, stepping toward her.

Bel shrank away, her tail between her legs. She turned her head to the side and looked at him out of the corners of her eyes, as if ashamed of her actions.

"Bel," he said and made a dart toward her.

She skittered off down the quay, stopped, and looked back.

"Come on, girl. Come on," he called, his voice quavering with tension.

Bel slunk away, farther down the quayside, and then looked over her shoulder at him.

"Leo, the tide's on the turn. We have to go. Now," the captain called.

He looked up and saw the two sailors standing on deck, the ropes in their hands, ready to haul up the gangplank.

"Bel," he tried again, taking a few steps. Bel backed away.

"Please, girl."

She was the last living link with his past life. If he went without her, he would have nothing. It would all be left behind. The friends he'd made. His family. Poland.

"Leo!" the captain called.

Mama. Papa. Dorota. Alexsy. Stefan. Maria. Jozef. Frederyk. Helena. The new brother or sister that he might never know. All of them.

"Bel!" he cried.

She stayed there, a dark, stubborn, unmoving shape that would not come with him.

"Last chance, Leo!" the captain said.

The gangplank began to scrape on the dockside as the two sailors hauled it up.

He took one last look at Bel and then dashed toward the ship. He ran up the gangplank and jumped onto the deck.

The captain tapped him on the shoulder. "You can stay on deck and watch until we're out at sea, and then the boatswain will show you where you'll sleep. I'll see you tomorrow."

The deck began to vibrate as the engine throbbed into life, driving the propeller. Men on the quayside untied the ropes, and the ship began to glide away from the land.

Now Bel came running along the quay, in and out of the shadows, tracking the ship as it moved downriver. He couldn't call to her. He could do nothing. He had made a decision, and now he was being borne away—alone, from everything he knew, toward whatever lay ahead.

Bel stopped eventually. He stared back at where she was standing until the ship rounded a bend, and she was gone.

It grew darker and darker, and he lost sight of the land they were passing until a flashing lighthouse showed a long spit of sandy dunes. Then the pitch and swell of the boat told him that they were out of the river and onto the immense sea. White-capped waves raced past below him.

Then someone was by his side. He turned and looked at a boy perhaps a year or two older than himself. The wind was tugging at the boy's hair, whipping it across his face. He pulled a striped woolly cap out of his pocket and jammed it on his head.

"Mateusz," the boy said.

"Leo."

They shook hands.

"You've fallen on your feet here, Leo," Mateusz said. "You're on the best damned ship, with the best damned crew, with the best damned captain on the whole seven seas. And don't you forget it."

Leo smiled, and Mateusz gave him a friendly punch on the arm. Then he strode away and climbed some steps to the upper deck.

Behind the ship, the glow from the lights of Danzig was fading.

Ahead, the ship was sailing into inky darkness.

The wind raced out of the black night, cutting into Leo and chilling him. But exciting him too. The prow of the boat was slicing through the waves with a thump and a hiss. He could see nothing, but he could feel the forward motion.

Somewhere in front of him was a new day. And, soon, far across the ocean lay America, and a new life.

"We're on our way, Tom," he said out loud. "We're on our way."

About the Author

Nigel Hinton was born in 1941 during an air raid in Britain. He is the author of eighteen books in the United Kingdom, and he has won numerous awards. *Walk the Wild Road* is the first time he has ever used his family history when crafting a novel.